Dead Balance

By
Gary Wayne Clark

Discover other titles on Amazon by
Gary Wayne Clark.

I0664898

Publisher's Note

This is a work of fiction and may not be suitable for all ages. The names, characters, places, languages, and incidents are either a product of my imagination or are used fictitiously. Any resemblance to actual persons, living or dead, business establishments, events, or locales is entirely coincidental. No part of this book may be reproduced, stored, performed, or transmitted by any means—whether auditory, graphic, mechanical, or electronic—without the written permission of both the publisher and author, except in the case of brief excerpts used in critical articles and reviews. Unauthorized reproduction of any part of this work is illegal and is punishable by law.

Author's Note

Through the power of genetic engineering, artificial intelligence, and sleep deprivation, this story sprang from my imagination, error-free. However, the reality of my fictional world would not be plausible if not riddled with human fallibility—some relatively minor and insignificant, others glaring and cataclysmic. To pay homage to this immutable truth, random, purposeful errors have been inserted to enhance the experience of my alternate reality.

Dedication

For Boo Bear

Honoo3itooné3en.
Nühü3é3en.
Hiiwóónhehe', tenéi'éíhin.

Prologue

In a remote mountain cabin along the Continental Divide, a disabled veteran known only as "Radio" closed the chat room on his computer and rolled his wheelchair across the room to the scanner. Rotating the frequency knob, he rubbed his eyes and glanced at the weather station mounted on the window outside.

3:05 PM, 20 degrees below zero.

A garbled voice crackled on his police scanner between the bursts of static.

"Sir, we've got another dead body. Well, at least part of one."

"Crap," he shivered, thinking about the bone-chilling cold outside. "Damn idiots, can't even get the frickin' time right."

Something didn't add up; the dispatcher's timestamp was 6:05 PM, not 3:05 PM. He glanced at the digital readout on the scanner and blinked. "Government bureaucrats," he mumbled, "wasting my tax money. Ought to fire the lot of them. Sheriff's Department? Department of frickin' idiots, that's what they are."

Noting the time discrepancy and the contents of the call in his log, Radio tightened the tattered fatigue jacket draped across his shoulders. He slumped down in his wheelchair, closed his eyes, and tried to doze off.

"Dead body…at least part of one," he muttered. "Frickin' morons."

Chapter 01: Kill Me Again

Winter along the Continental Divide can be harsh and unforgiving for a trained outdoorsman; for the untrained, it often proves deadly. Many a backcountry adventurer has become disoriented in whiteout conditions and wandered off the trail, only to have his body recovered in the spring thaw.

It was almost dark when two hikers with snowshoes from the Spirit Lake Trailhead stumbled upon a torn backpack at a remote campsite near Dead Horse Canyon. While one hiker was rummaging through the backpack, the other called out nervously after scanning the area for signs of life. "I've got a creepy feeling about this…"

"Me too," the second hiker echoed. "Over there!" He pointed at drag marks in the snow leading into the woods. "Bad karma, man."

As the hiker turned away from the trail, he tripped over something, landing a face plant in a snowdrift. He reached down and picked up an object under his boot, let out a shriek, and pitched it into the air.

"What the hell was that?"

"A foot! A human foot!"

Panicked, the hikers scrambled back down the mountain to find cell service. Retracing their steps in the snow, they staggered back to the trailhead, got a few bars on their cell phones, and managed to reach the authorities at 6:01 PM, frantically relaying their story.

"I'll call the sheriff; stay there until she arrives," the

dispatcher instructed. "She will need to take your statements."

"OK, OK. How long?"

"She's thirty minutes out."

"Jesus! That thing is still out there, man! What if…"

"Stay calm, sir. You're in the warming hut at the trailhead, right?"

"Yeah."

"That old log cabin was built by the park service a hundred years ago. You'll be safe inside, just keep the door barred. I'll message our CSi; he's not that far away."

"OK."

"And we'll need that foot for evidence. Do you have it with you?"

"No frickin' way, man!" the hiker screamed. "I tossed that thing and ran like a bat out of hell! I'm never going back to that creep show."

Chapter 02: Dark Talk

Logan Lone Bear Tuu'awta pushed back from his *Dark Talk* chat room, a late-night cyber hangout for local conspiracy theorists, ghost hunters, and insomniacs. He peered out the window and rubbed his mug; it was as cold as the icy wind howling outside, clanging the broken shutters of the Timberline Tea Haus.

"Need a warm up, love?" the waitress sighed as she brushed against his shoulder.

The hour was late and they were alone, as they were most winter nights in the deserted tourist town of Deadraven, nestled high in the Rocky Mountains.

"Thanks, I'm almost done," Logan said as he hit the Enter key. "Off you go."

He glanced up and once again fell into the most beautiful brown eyes he'd ever seen in his life. Holding eye contact for a moment, he clumsily slid his mug along the table for a refill and tapped three times on the teapot the waitress held next to her apron. "They say that eyes are the windows to the soul. A man could fall into yours and never return...and never want to."

"A man could," the waitress shot back playfully as she pulled away, "but a boy shouldn't." She paused a moment, smiled, and then leaned in close over Logan's shoulder, scanning his words of wisdom. "Hmm...What deep, spiritual enigma do you have for your loyal minions of the blogosphere this evening?"

She tapped an icon on the screen, and the computer's text to speech application read Logan's latest missives aloud.

Most people live their lives wishing, hoping, fearing what the future will bring. Someone once said that the only thing known about the future is that it's unknown. But what if it wasn't...unknown, that is? What if you were granted a brief glimpse into the future? Would you take it?'

"Heavy thoughts before bedtime," the waitress observed.

As she watched the return comments fill the computer screen, she glanced down at Logan closing his eyes.

"Looks like you hit a nerve. Is it always like this?"

"Yeah," Logan sighed. "Seems there's always someone who wants my advice, wants me to tell them what they should do."

"And do you? Give them advice, I mean?"

"No. I have enough trouble navigating my own thoughts. I can't see into someone else's future."

The waitress studied Logan's face as his head lay peacefully on the table.

"Well, I've looked into your future, and it doesn't included any more tea tonight." She batted her eyes as Logan glanced up at her. "But a boy with your talents already knew that, didn't you?"

Before Logan could mount a defense to his manhood, the distinct sound of a police dispatch message on his computer blurted out an interruption to his protest.

"11-44 @ N 40° 18' 47.5" W 105° 38' 53.6" . 11-98 L Spirit Lake Trailhead ASAP."

Logan snapped out of his momentary infatuation. "Ten-four," he responded, taking a last sip of tea. "OK if I leave this here?" Logan asked, sliding his computer behind the bar.

"No problem. I'll keep an eye on it."

"Thanks, I'm traveling light."

"By the way, are you still bird-dogging for Search and Rescue?" the waitress asked.

"Sometimes, I'm more recovery than rescue these days," Logan quipped as he scanned the empty room and dug into his pocket for a crinkled dollar bill. "I've got a new gig with the po po. Someone's got to keep the lights on around here." He smiled and yawned.

"Ah, and thank you, kind sir," the waitress retorted, sliding the tip into her apron. "Your generosity is only exceeded by your…intellect. Come back any night; I'm always open for you."

"I'm counting on that." Logan smiled.

Chapter 03: Bad Karma

Logan arrived at the Spirit Lake Trailhead warming hut to meet the hysterical hikers. He identified himself as a CSi liaison with the Sheriff's Department and tried to calm them down, assuring them they would be safe now. After listening to their story, he asked them to wait inside for the sheriff and set out up the rocky terrain in the direction of the campsite the hikers had described.

Scrambling along the trail as fast as he could, he knew that what was left of the hiker's footprints would disappear quickly in the wind-driven snow. In thirty minutes, the trail would be gone.

Reaching the remote campsite, Logan scanned the scene with his flashlight. The chaotic combination of random tracks on the ground and the severed foot dangling from a tree branch gave him an eerie feeling.

"This is…bad medicine," he exhaled, as he grabbed a stick and poked the frozen body part above his head in the tree until it dislodged and fell to the ground.

Logan knelt down, shined his flashlight on the severed foot, and studied the dried blood on the jagged lacerations. He stood and panned the surroundings. Illuminating the snow-covered drag marks near the tree line, he followed them fifty yards into the thick brush.

"Bad," he shook his head, "would be an understatement."

Between Search and Rescue and his stint as an alcoholic coroner's unofficial assistant, Logan had seen some gruesome crime scenes in his young life: cliff divers, stabbings, car crashes, self-immolation, and all varieties of gunshots, but this scene was beyond horrific. In a small clearing across a rocky crevice, there were scattered parts of a body, a body that had been ripped apart, strewn about, and partially consumed. He bent down and touched a mangled torso where a beating heart had once been, offering a prayer.

"Go with the Creator, my friend. Your suffering in this world is over."

Sensing something was out of balance, Logan stood and slowly rotated. He closed his eyes and inhaled deeply as he sought to absorb this place of death into his mind.

The forest became a snowy blur, a chaotic view of broken branches, overturned rocks, and scattered limbs. A hungry animal sniffed the air and smelled blood, drool dripping down its fangs. Following the scent, the animal followed the kill through the woods, soon to claim it for its own. On a windy, snow-driven, rocky outcrop just ahead, there was a low growl, a mad rush, and the carnage ensued.

The screech of an owl echoed down the canyon as a cold breeze startled Logan back to reality. He exhaled, opened his eyes, and a shiver ran down his spine.

Something dark and unnatural had been here—something evil. It was an evil Logan had felt once before, long ago. He blinked his eyes and the bone-chilling feeling dissipated—it was gone. Taking a deep breath, he refocused and resumed cataloging the rest of the crime scene in his mind. There was more forensic evidence to be examined, but he'd seen enough; it was time to report in.

'*You're late to the party, Sheriff,*' Logan messaged on his police radio.

'*Almost there,*' Sheriff Billie Sue Martin sent a text from the trailhead. '*Paperwork.*'

The sheriff finished taking statements from the hikers at the trailhead and made her way up the mountain to the campsite. She looked around as she followed the snow-covered trail of peeled tree bark marked by Logan into the brush, meeting him in the rocky clearing.

"Damn it," she exhaled, scanning the body parts on the ground. "I've seen picnics gone wrong, but this one takes the cake. What the hell happened here?"

"Wallet identifies the victim as one Dr. Malcolm Kennedy. At first glance, it looks like he was alone, surprised a bear, and got the worst of it."

The sheriff bent down to examine what was left of the figure on the ground. She poked a mound of human flesh with a stick, stood up, and scanned the clearing.

"OK, when Yogi snatches a *pic-a-nic* basket from a camper, that's funny. When Yogi eats a camper, that's not so funny. Poor son of a bitch, I had a bad feeling on this one, so I called the park service."

"You're a team player, Sheriff."

"Their jurisdiction. Besides, we've got new regulations with the park service. Any deaths that might be '*wildlife related,*' we get assigned a '*bear buddy.*' Don't want to spook the tourists, you know."

Another flashlight flickered from the campsite below. It was the park ranger alerted by the sheriff.

"Over here!" Billie Sue waved her lamp and called from the crime scene.

The ranger made her way from the darkness into the rocky clearing, scanned the bloody corpse in the snow, and let out a whistle.

"Looks like we're going to need your…cooperation on this one, Ranger," the sheriff stated calmly. "On the down-low."

"You can count on me, Sheriff. What do you think happened here?"

The sheriff turned to Logan.

"You said, 'looks like a hiker surprised a bear, at first glance.' What did you mean by that?"

"The bear wasn't the first guest at the party; that's what I mean. This guy was already dead before the organs in his chest were eaten and his arms removed."

"Already dead?"

"If the bear didn't kill him, how did he die?" the ranger asked.

"Suicide," Logan responded.

"What leads you to that conclusion?" The sheriff scratched her head.

"Simple," Logan answered, bending down to the body. "If you were being eaten alive, Sheriff, you'd have fought back, wouldn't you?" Logan pointed to the severed limbs on the ground with a stick.

"Like a son of a bitch."

"Exactly. But our victim has no defensive wounds on the arms or hands. No teeth marks on the limbs, only on the torso."

"What about the foot?"

"I'm guessing that was the consolation prize to the loser in this tug-of-war."

"Really? Anything else?" the sheriff queried.

"Yes, he died somewhere else. The body was moved here." Logan stood up, wielding his stick around the crime scene.

"OK…"

"The drag marks from the campsite through the

woods to here are mostly over rocks," the ranger observed. "I can't get a track off them. You sure a bear didn't kill him?"

"Quite sure," Logan answered.

"And it wasn't a heart attack?" Sheriff Martin questioned. "We get a lot of those at this altitude, you know."

"This was a suicide," Logan stated, "he hanged himself. And not here; the original crime scene is somewhere else on the mountain."

"Hanged himself?" The sheriff scratched her head again. "Before the bear ate him?"

"Without a doubt. He's got rope burns on his neck," Logan said, bending down to point out the marks with his stick.

"Yeah, now I see them," the sheriff sighed. She leaned over and picked up a piece of flesh, placing it in an evidence bag. "That sure appears to be what happened, all right. Case solved, tag it and bag it. Let's call it a night."

Logan glanced over at the ranger as she nodded her agreement with the sheriff.

As they made their way back to the campsite, the sheriff caught up with the ranger.

"For the record, you got any more observations, bear buddy?"

"Yeah," the ranger articulated. "Another flatlander climbs the mountain to get close to nature. Well, he did, all right."

"What is it they say to attract tourists to this town?" Logan asked.

"It's a wonderful day here at the Deadraven Winter Festival," Sheriff Martin repeated robotically as she switched into marketing mode. "A place where you can relax, listen to the voice of the mountain, enjoy nature, and discover your inner self."

"Discover your inner self," Logan countered. "Or kill it. A Rocky Mountain holiday—It's to die for."

"They should add that to the travel brochure!" the ranger laughed.

"Yes, I think I'll suggest that...*not*" the sheriff stopped for a moment on the trail. "You know, all joking aside, there's one thing that still bothers me."

"What?" the ranger asked.

"Who moved the body?"

"That's easy," the ranger offered. "A mountain lion probably found the hanging dead guy and carried him up here to hide her meal. Bear shows up, steals the kill. A black bear can smell blood up to twenty-five miles away. When the bear found the body, he chased away the mountain lion."

"That would explain the lack of drag marks," Logan added. "A lion would carry her meal, not drag it. And from the puncture wounds on the back of the neck, I'd say the lion got to him first."

"Missed that," Sheriff Martin confessed. "You never see lions coming because they always attack from behind, don't they?"

"Exactly," the ranger agreed. "Those canines clamped on the back of your neck? That's the first clue they're stalking you."

"What's the second clue?"

"Doesn't matter, you're dead."

"Predators and scavengers, thinning the human herd," Sheriff Martin stated.

"It's nature's way," Logan added.

The ranger pointed at a stand of dead lodgepole pines.

"Circle of life, Sheriff, animals need protein. With the beetle kill, drought, and wildfires, there's a lot less prey up here to support the predators. They've all got to eat."

The ranger whipped out her logbook.

"So, for the official paperwork, Sheriff, how do we want to record tonight's adventure?"

"Let's see, either a tourist committed suicide, was partially eaten by a lion, and then finished off by a bear, or a hiker fell down in the woods. Let's go with the clumsy hiker for the report, unless the family requests an autopsy. This one's a closed casket anyway, best to let sleeping dogs lie. Now help me get what's left of Dr. Kennedy here bagged up before we get any more scavengers looking for a meal. I'll call Search and Rescue in the morning for a sweep of the nearby trails to see if we can find where this guy punched out, but in this weather, I'm betting we'll never know."

"Works for me," the ranger closed her logbook and studied Logan's face.

"Have we ever met before?" she asked. "You seem familiar to me."

"Can't say that we have," Logan replied casually. "Unless you've been in juvie."

"We've all got a past," the ranger laughed. "I'm not here to judge."

"You keep an eye on Yogi for me," the sheriff interrupted. "He's a big boy, and I don't need him helping any more hikers fall down, not even frozen dead guys. Bad for tourism, you know."

"Will do, Sheriff."

Back at the trailhead, Logan waved as the ranger drove away. In addition to the strange feeling he'd experienced at the crime scene, his mind was still processing some other inconsistencies.

"Something doesn't add up here."

"The torn hiker's backpack at the campsite?" the sheriff interrupted.

"I didn't find one."

"Neither did I," the sheriff echoed. "And the second?"

"From the size of those paw prints, that was no black bear."

"Yeah, he's bigger than any bear I've ever seen up here," the sheriff nodded, "as big as a Kodiak."

"And the way it ripped apart the body…" Logan paused, shaking a memory from his head. "It wasn't his first trip to the buffet."

"No, it wasn't," the sheriff acknowledged as she added a note in her unofficial log for the coroner: *Potential man-eater, handle Code Red.*

Chapter 04: Truth Detector

Slumped into an overstuffed sofa in the garage lounge of High Country Cycles, Logan's mind was still tumbling over the brutal crime scene he'd witnessed in the National Park at Spirit Lake. Parsing the comments from last night's webcast of his *Truth Detector* blog, a one-line entry caught his attention. Buried amidst the usual expletive rants, late-night confessions, and Bigfoot sightings, this one hit him like a punch in the gut.

'I know what happened at Spirit Lake last night.'

Logan sat up as he reread the comment from a visitor to his blog labeled only as "Radio." His heartbeat accelerated as he typed a return message: *'What do you know?'*

After several seconds, an answer appeared: *'A hiker fell down in the woods, the end. Not.'*

'How do you know that?' Logan messaged.

'Not here, too many eyes. Meet at these coordinates: 40° 15' 16.9" W 105° 36' 57", IRL.'

Logan paused for a moment to reflect on the conversation. How could this anonymous stranger named Radio know what happened at Spirit Lake? Probably another whacko lurking around his chat room, seeking attention…There was no shortage of them these days. He shrugged and rummaged between the pizza boxes and beer bottles on the coffee table to dig out a video game controller. Clicking on the big screen, he immediately was catapulted into the pilot seat of a

Longbow Apache assault helicopter, dodging buildings, and anti-aircraft fire on a mission to rescue a fallen soldier from behind enemy lines. Just as he navigated the chopper down through a smoke-filled landing zone, the metal clang of a wrench hitting the concrete floor abruptly broke his train of thought.

It was Cody Winston, the owner of the motorcycle shop and arguably the best two-wheel grease monkey and video game chopper pilot west of the Mississippi. Rumor had it she'd been in every jail from here to Juarez, riding a tricked-out Indian and fronting her punk rock band. The wrench that bounced past his foot confirmed why: Other than internal combustion engines, her knack for bad timing was renowned.

"Sorry about that, man," Cody apologized, noticing the apprehension on Logan's face. "What's got your panties in a knot?"

" 'Strange things done beneath the midnight sun...' up at Spirit Lake last night," Logan began quoting a poem from his youth.

"Stranger than finding a '36 Knucklehead in the river at the bottom of Devil's Backbone?" Cody snapped back, pulling a tarp off a crashed motorcycle in her workshop.

"What the hell?" Logan gasped, leaping up to view the prized Harley.

"Tell me about it," Cody sighed. "I've always wanted to feel my legs around a Knucklehead. Thought I'd won the lottery fishing this baby out of the river until some weekend warrior flyboy shows up to claim it. Said he ditched on Dead Man's Curve last week; now he wants it back. After I risked life and limb crawling down those cliffs to bring this carcass back from the dead."

"Well, technically, it is his," Logan counseled.

"Maybe it is…and maybe it isn't. I told him it's mine under maritime salvage law."

"Maritime salvage…from a river?"

"There's legal precedent."

"Where did you come up with that?"

"The Internet. They can't put anything that's not true on the Internet."

"What did he say to that?"

"That my creative claim was bogus; he still wants his bike back. Oh, and he wants to go out with me."

"Really? Is he hot?"

"Yeah, he's stone cold, brother, but that's not the point."

"So what *is* the point?"

"It's all about the dance, my friend. The thrill of the chase…the push and shove of…*amore*. Flyboy wants? Flyboy's got to give. Nobody wraps their legs around my Knucklehead for free."

"So you're holding his bike hostage?"

"Damn straight I am. At least until I get a little something for my trouble."

Before the romantic salvage argument could continue, the garage door flung open and in strode Raven Thunder Sky. She was a young, slender, beautiful Indian girl with two long braids of black hair drooping over her shoulders.

"We've been looking for you," Raven announced, as she wedged herself onto the sofa between Cody and Logan. Glancing over at the crumpled motorcycle that seemed to hold everyone's attention, she locked eyes with Logan for a second.

"The bike can wait," Raven announced. "We want to hear what happened at Spirit Lake last night."

Logan held her gaze for a moment, and then broke it off.

"It seems we've got a new predator roaming the high country."

"And that's a problem because…?"

"Because this one seems to have acquired a taste for human flesh."

Cody and Raven listened intently as Logan recounted the events of the night, and the recent contact with the mysterious connection known only as Radio.

"What do you think this shadow knows?" Cody inquired.

"I don't know, but I intend to find out."

Cody slid over to her desk of computer screens and did a quick geo-location on Radio's coordinates from the blog post.

"This dude is high, man," she whistled. "His transmitter beacon clocks in above 14,000 feet."

"I'm coming with you," Raven pronounced as she stood up. "There's a storm blowing in, and you'll never make it up there on foot. Besides, my horses know every trail on the mountain."

Logan started to protest, but realized that hiking alone to the rim of the world in the dead of winter was a bad idea. Raven had grown up riding bareback along the Continental Divide with her grandfather, and she did know the terrain up there like the back of her hand. Yes, he needed her, and she knew it.

"OK, princess, let's saddle up," he relented. "Let's go see what the Radio knows."

Chapter 05: Timberline

After loading the horses, Raven and Logan started the slow, windy climb up the one-lane gravel road into Continental Divide National Park. The icy trail was treacherous in winter; one slip could lead to a thousand-foot plunge over the edge of the ridgeline to the jagged rocks below. They rode in silence as the diesel engine of the four-by-four chugged away under the weight of the horse trailer carrying Raven's two black Percherons, finally arriving after several hours at the Wild River Gorge Trailhead.

"End of the line, boys," Raven announced. She dropped the tailgate and backed the horses out of the trailer. "Time to go to work."

It was just before sunset, and the snow was falling gently on the narrow trail as they made their way deep into the woods, the rhythmic clopping of the horses' hooves on the loose rocks echoing down the ravine. A cold wind swirled in the pine trees, and the temperature dropped quickly as night fell, reminding Logan and Raven of a time when they had been alone on this mountain before as children, an adventure that neither of them ever would forget.

"He's not mad at you," Raven blurted out.

Logan didn't answer.

"He knows you're back, and he wants to see you…Correction, he *needs* to see you." Raven stopped her mount squarely in the trail and faced Logan, determined to make her point.

"Why would I do that?"

"Because I promised him you would."

"You shouldn't make promises you can't keep," Logan said softly as he guided his horse around her and headed up the trail. "You know I can't change the past."

As they rode on in silence, Logan leaned back in his saddle and gazed up at the last rays of light streaming over the mountain peaks; it soon would be dark. For a brief moment, his mind drifted back to another time, a time he had tried desperately to forget. A cold wind ruffled Logan's oilskin duster, snapping him back to reality.

"We're almost there," he announced as he checked the coordinates on his GPS.

Up ahead, the deep forest trail ended abruptly as they emerged into the moonlight above the broken clouds. They'd reached the alpine tree line, a rocky, windswept tundra under snowpack that was inhospitable in summer and nearly impassable in winter.

Logan and Raven dismounted, giving the Percherons a rest. Going any higher on horseback would be impossible; they would need to lead the horses from this point to avoid stumbling on the frozen trail and plunging to their deaths on the sharp rocks below.

Raven squinted as she scanned the rocky outcroppings along the tree line.

"Over there, five hundred yards...looks like an old cabin wedged into the cliff face."

Logan released the lead rope for the horses and scrambled over the icy rocks toward the cabin.

"OK, shadow man, let's hear what you've got to say."

Following the careful footsteps Logan left in the snow, Raven led the Percherons single file along the narrow rock scrabble trail. One of the horses stumbled and sent a rockslide cascading down the mountain, echoing through the winds.

"Easy, boys." Raven hugged the crag's edge as she assured the horses. "Don't look down; we're almost there."

"Over here," Logan called out, waving his hand. "There's a run in up here where we can tie the horses."

As Raven rounded the last curve of the narrow trail, she found Logan wedged inside a rocky crevice beneath a makeshift roof of pine branches, stroking the nose of a fuzzy mule munching some hay.

"Well, it's not as cozy as their barn stall," Raven said as she led the horses in, "but they'll be warm enough huddled together out of the wind."

Logan and Raven made their way between the boulders to the cabin, climbed onto the rough-hewn log porch, and banged on the door until a flicker of light appeared through the window. They heard a creaking sound slowly approaching across the old wooden floor, and then the rustic door swung open wide. There, in front of them, was a disheveled man in a wheelchair, wearing a tattered military uniform and holding a double-barrel shotgun and a beer on his lap.

"About time you got here," the man scolded as he adjusted his headphones and rolled back into the cabin. "Any later, and I was locking down for the night."

Logan stepped into the cabin, but Raven was frozen on the threshold, staring at the crusty man in the wheelchair.

"Don't get many visitors up here," the man called from across the room, spinning his wheelchair around to lock eyes on Raven. "Well, look here. Who is this lovely young lady?"

Realizing that her eyes were fixated on the wheelchair, Raven broke her awkward gaze, entered the cabin, and closed the door.

"What happened to my legs? That what's eating you?" Radio offered in response to the quickly hidden expression on Raven's face.

"I didn't mean to...stare," Raven blushed.

The man known as Radio rolled over to study her face in the dim light of the fire.

"IED. Fallujah," he laughed as he circled her. "Blew off most of my right leg. So, what the hell? Government just issued me a new one."

"Then how did you get...up here?"

Radio smiled. "On my beast of burden, just like you. 'Chip,' I call him. He's part mule, part mountain goat."

"OK..." Raven paused. "*Why* are you here?"

"None of our business," Logan interrupted. "We're just here to..."

"At ease, soldier!" Radio snapped back. "I don't mind sharing; that's why I contacted you."

The man rolled over to the fire and poked it, sending sparks up the chimney. After chugging what was left of his beer, he crushed the can and tossed it into a barrel of empties by the fire. Radio stared into the fire for a moment, seeming to reflect on some distant memory.

"When the war was over for me, I kind of dropped out. My VA shrink said I had PTSD and some kind of *'anger management'* issues. Anger management? Crap, they tell you over there, *'trust no one and kill anything that moves.'* Beat it in your head, they do. They drop you in some foreign country, and you just do what you're trained to do: kill people, I mean, lots of them. Men, women, children…hell, it don't matter. As long as you think they're trying to kill you, they're the enemy. It's kill or be killed. Then they expect you to come home, flip a switch in your head, and get a job selling real estate to some pimply-faced adolescents that can't even find where you've been on a map. Damn kids don't know what it's like to be talking to a buddy one moment, and the next watch him blown apart right in front of you. They don't know what it's like to look into the terrified eyes of a man with his guts hanging out of his chest, screaming in pain as he bleeds to death in your arms. They don't know…what I know."

Radio paused for a moment and looked out the window and sighed. "So…I came to this mountaintop to find myself."

"How's that going for you?" Raven inquired.

"So far?" Radio laughed. "Can't say I like what I've found." He rolled over to the kitchen. "But that's a whole other story. Want some tea? I dry the flowers myself."

Raven studied the numerous containers of dried leaves on the kitchen shelves. She recognized some of the plants as rare alpine tundra flowers she'd seen her grandfather use in his ceremonies. Others, she'd never seen before.

"Sure, I'll have a cup."

"I tune into your little show," Radio said as he turned to Logan. "You know, on my satellite link. Conspiracy man, don't trust anyone, do you?"

"I trust," Logan said. "But first, I verify."

"I heard that," Radio scoffed, rolling over to poke the fire. "Just because you're paranoid doesn't mean they're not out to get you. We're cut from the same cloth, you and me. You're the Truth Detector; lots of people listen to you. Hang on your every word, they do. Well, I'm a truth detector too, you see. Only difference between you and me is that no one listens to me."

"You said you knew what happened up at Spirit Lake," Logan interrupted. "I'm listening."

"Wait," Raven interrupted. "I brought you a gift." She reached into her jacket and pulled out a small dried flower bundle. "You might like these with your tea. I picked them myself."

"Why thank you," Radio blushed. "Visitors and a present. Quite a day."

"One should always offer a gift *before* asking a favor." Raven shot a glance toward Logan. "It's tradition."

"My bad," Logan acknowledged. "Seems I've forgotten my manners. Now, you said you knew what happened at Spirit Lake. What would make you say that?"

"Want the long version or the short version?"

"Whatever you're willing to share."

"Guess it'll be the long version, then." Radio scratched his beard as he looked out the window of his one-room cabin. "Storm's a coming. You won't be heading down the mountain tonight."

Raven and Logan sat down in front of the fire on the floor as Radio lit up a joint, inhaled deeply, and then offered it to Raven.

"No, thanks, I'm trying to quit," Raven said.

"No worries," Radio exhaled, blowing a smoke ring across the room. "Ever hear of Aokigahara?"

"No…" Logan exchanged a glance with Raven as she shook her head.

"It's a suicide forest at the base of Mt. Fuji. Quiet little place in the wilderness, people go to enjoy nature and commune with God. Oh, and then they kill themselves. Goodbye, cruel world."

"Why?" Logan asked, leaning forward.

"Why indeed. No one knows for sure. It's like something from the dark side draws them to that mountain, puts a rope around their neck, and then shoves them over the edge. *Sayonara*."

"That's creepy," Raven injected.

"What's that got to do with what happened at Spirit Lake?" Logan pressed.

"If you ask me, it seems to me like we've got our own little suicide forest right here on this mountain. You have to dig, but I did my research. People been coming here for years to take a cliff dive, hang themselves, or just blow their frickin' heads off."

As Radio's words washed over his mind, Logan thought about all the bodies he'd encountered with Search and Rescue.

"OK, I hear you. Go on."

"I heard Indians won't live up here, you know, too smart for that. Others say this place has some kind of bad juju. Whatever it is, been going on up here for a while—way before I crashed this party. Five to ten bodies a year, people offing themselves, regular as clockwork. It's like some mystical toll the mountain charges for revealing her beauty. Kind of like that spider that eats her mate after sex."

"What you say is true; I've seen it in Search and…Recovery. But as you said, it's been going on for a while. Why did you contact me now?"

"Because something has changed. Seems to me like the mountain is pissed off for some reason and for starters has just jacked up her toll."

"What do you think it means?" Raven said as she

shot a glance at Logan.

"Whatever it means, young lady, we've got corpses stacking up like cordwood out there."

"That would explain…" Logan started.

"Wait!" Radio interrupted. "You hear that?"

"What?"

"Probably nothing," Radio sighed. "I hear a lot of nothing these days."

"Back to the beginning," Logan redirected. "You said you knew what happened up at Spirit Lake."

"I did."

"What did you mean?"

"That deal I heard, out in the ether, the other night up at Spirit Lake? *A hiker fell down in the woods?*"

"Go on."

"Who do they think they're kidding? A guy hangs himself, a bear eats him, and they think no one will notice?" Radio leaned back in his wheelchair, closing his eyes. "Not good for tourism, they say. Suppress the bad news, they whisper. Bury the lead. Hell, bury the story and the body."

"How did you know about that? About what happened at Spirit Lake, I mean."

"Because she told me," Radio said softly, pointing a shaking finger at his scanner.

"She?"

"Yeah, she tells me about that kind of crap all the time."

"What?"

"Suicides, murders, bears eatin' people…She tells me, over there, on the scanner."

Just then, a police dispatch interrupted their discussion: "We've got a dog running off leash downtown again. Any officer in the vicinity, respond."

"You mean the sheriff's office dispatcher?"

"No! Not her! The other one!"

Logan and Raven looked at each other, confused.

"What...other one?"

"The one that comes on before her, before the sheriff lady!" Radio rubbed his eyes in frustration and popped open another beer. "Her handle's 'Guardian.' She's usually on channel six, but she jumps all around. The sheriff lady's on channel one—always on channel one!"

Logan looked at Raven, raising his eyebrows.

"She's driving me insane! Always telling me some bad crap's gonna happen, then it does."

"OK, OK." Logan tried to get Radio to slow down.

"I tried unplugging that damn scanner, but the messages still come...in my head. They won't stop."

"Back to Spirit Lake," Logan said, trying to understand.

"That's when it happened again! She told me about the dead guy hanging himself and then getting eaten."

"*When* did she tell you?"

"Before! I told you, before the sheriff lady made the dispatch call!"

"Before?"

"Yeah, before that son of a bitch hanged himself—way before."

"And the bear attack happened *after* you got the call from this...Guardian, you called her?"

"Freaky, huh?" Radio shook his head and took another hit. "Why does she lay that heavy trip on me? It's like I'm in some frequency-hopping time warp!"

"Have you told the sheriff your story?"

"Hell yeah!" Radio perked up. "Called it in, the

Spirit Lake deal, just like the other times."

"'That's all?'they said. 'OK, we'll look into it. Now stay off this channel, it's just for emergencies.'"

"Liars. Never do crap about anything. Said I should stop drinking and keep off their frickin' airwaves. Hell's bells, man, all I drink is tea. And a little beer now and then, but that's just to dull the pain in my leg. I stay alert when I'm on duty, twenty-four-seven. I try to help them out, and they act like they own the frickin' airwaves! Government don't own the airwaves, you know, and they sure as hell don't give a burnt mule about the truth. Nobody wants to hear the truth these days…except you. You seek the truth, don't you?"

Radio rolled forward and looked into Logan's eyes. "That's why I called you, Truth Detector."

"You have to admit," Logan said, "that's a pretty hard story to believe."

"A frickin' conspiracy is what it is—government cover-up. They're all in on it, you know."

"I hear you, my friend," Logan counseled. "The truth is a stranger to most. But do you have any hard evidence of this…conspiracy?"

"Well, shit yeah, Sherlock. Why do you think I called this meeting? I make a log and record all my scanner calls."

Radio rolled over to his communication desk, punched a few buttons, and played back the voice he called "Guardian." Logan listened intently as he fumbled in his pocket and hit Record on his phone.

When the voice finally stopped, Radio let out a sigh of relief. "It's getting late, soldier. Reveille comes pretty early up here. There's two sleeping bags over there on the dresser; you guys can crash by the fire."

Raven tossed a sleeping bag to Logan in front of

the hearth as they settled down to reflect on the night's adventure.

"Well, what do you think, *Truth Detector?*" Raven said softly.

"I think that's a whole lot of *truth* to process," Logan whispered. "What do you think?"

"I think we should get some sleep and an early start down the mountain tomorrow. And on the way, I think you should stop and talk with Ten Bears."

"Why?" Logan said as he closed his eyes.

"I told you already. Because he needs to see you."

"Is that all?" Logan mumbled as he closed his eyes.

"Not exactly…that frequency-hopping babble our PTSD friend just spilled?"

"Yeah?"

"Ten Bears has heard it, too."

Chapter 06: Left-Hand

A cold winter wind whistled outside Radio's alpine cabin, gently banging the wooden shutters against the log windowsill. The dying embers of the fire glowed in the darkness, casting shadows that conjured illusory ghost dancers floating across the ceiling. Raven and Radio quickly had drifted off to sleep, but Logan was wide awake, staring into the fire. His mind drifted back to the last time he was on this mountain, and the distant pain that throbbed like a dull knife in his heart.

Somewhere between the bitter memories and his dreams, Logan was eight years old again. His father was a ranger with the Tenth Mountain Division, off fighting some forgotten war in Pakistan, Afghanistan, or was it Kurdistan? *One of the 'stans, anyway*, he thought. Logan's dad was a decorated Indian warrior from the Rocky Mountains who had gone against tradition and married outside his tribe, a soft-spoken young nurse with crystal blue eyes who patched up his wounded body and captured his heart with her kindness and gentle touch on the battlefield.

Before the war, Logan's father was a Medicine Man, known by his tribe as Left-Hand, the descendent of a great Indian chief. As a boy, Left-Hand taught Logan the things he considered most valuable to pass on to a young warrior: to protect those who counted on him, to hear the inner voice of his spirit, and if need be, to kill.

As a military scout, Left-Hand did all these things

well until he and his K9 were blown to bits in a drone strike behind enemy lines that went terribly wrong. Some weekend warrior video game jockey in a lounge chair half a world away got an itchy trigger finger, and the brave scout who routinely risked his life to save innocent noncombatants in a forgotten part of the world from rape, murder, and genocide, was gone.

"Sorry, ma'am, the fog of war, you know. He was a patriot."

There was no parade, no ceremony, no newspaper article, no hero's welcome home. Not even a brief announcement on the PA system at Logan's school, just that tactless explanation and a flag-draped coffin was all that Logan and his mother ever received from the military.

The death of his father was traumatic enough, but it was the callous explanation of his senseless killing that destroyed his mother. As an outsider to her husband's tribe and an outcast to the local townspeople, she was left alone in her grief. His mother fell hard, crawled into a bottle, and never came out.

Because of Logan's ancestors, Raven's grandfather had taken him under his wing, continuing the teachings his father began, as a potential Medicine Man, and in the ways of the Ancient Ones. Logan and Raven spent many a late night around the campfire enthralled by the tales of Ten Bears.

"I have chosen you two to learn my medicine," Ten Bears announced one night as he puffed away on his long pipe, waving the smoke into circles around his face.

"Why?" Raven asked.

"Because someday there will come a time when I can no longer carry the Thunder Stick that stands guard on this mountain. When that day arrives, its medicine will be yours to wield."

Being children, Logan and Raven had both been confused and honored to accept the wisdom that Ten Bears entrusted to them. He shared stories of ancient spirits, mythical beasts, magical medicines and spells, but in exchange, demanded that to remain his apprentices, they each would need to prove themselves worthy.

"We begin with two rules," Ten Bears continued. "First, the powerful medicine of our ancestors that I teach you must be carefully guarded; you are to never disclose these secrets to another living soul. And second, that you always respect your ancestors and their sacred places. Disrespect for them will bring pain and suffering to us all."

Eager to learn the secret ways of the past, Logan and Raven promised that they always would abide by Ten Bears' rules. Little did they know that despite their pledge, this was a promise meant to be broken.

Playing hide-and-seek one day along the Continental Divide, Raven stumbled into a cave high on Thunderbird Mountain. Fascinated by the colorful petroglyphs lining the walls, she called to Logan, and he followed her along a narrow stone trail deep into the mountain. They didn't realize that by entering the cave of the Ancient Ones, they'd broken their promise to Ten Bears. More importantly, their actions on that day had set in motion a series of events that would rip apart their world and inevitably claim many lives. However, the strangest thing about their innocent transgression that day was that they didn't have to confess it to Ten Bears; as soon as they entered the sacred cave, somehow, he knew.

"It was a cold wind I felt on the mountain that day," Ten Bears lamented. "The day your promise was broken, and evil cast its shadow on this world."

Ten Bears was furious at them both.

In an attempt to shield Raven from her grandfather's wrath, Logan tried to assume complete responsibility for their accidental incursion. For some unknown reason, at the age of eight, Logan had already decided that he was, and always would be, Raven's protector.

"I am sorry; I have failed you," Logan confessed to Ten Bears. "I led Raven into the cave. I alone deserve whatever punishment you decide."

The judgment by Raven's grandfather was swift and final. His commandments had been broken, and for that, there could be no forgiveness. Logan understood that he was no longer worthy of spiritual training, and he would endure whatever punishment was coming, to spare Raven. "To protect those who counted on him," that was the mark of a warrior; that was what his father had taught him.

"You will leave this mountain," Ten Bears commanded.

Logan was devastated. Being denied the spiritual teachings of Ten Bears was bad enough, but as his fragile world spun out of control, it was about to get much worse. His mother hit rock bottom and was locked up for another drunken bender and fight at a local bar. She was a pariah, and no one stepped forward to post her bail. It was the third time in a month that his mom had an altercation; this time she'd punched out some coward for spitting on returning veterans as they exited a Greyhound bus, taunting them for being, "merciless criminals of an immoral war machine." Her husband had given his life in that immoral war for the freedom of others, including those cowards, and she just snapped.

"This time," the judge said, "it's three strikes and you're out; six months in jail."

The next day, Child Services showed up to take Logan into protective custody. Lacking any juvenile facilities in a remote mountain town, that meant being locked up in the county jail. After a week of incarceration for no crime of his own, Logan received a hearing. The same overworked judge who had tossed his mom in jail peered over a pile of paperwork on his desk. He asked Logan if there were any other family members or responsible parties who could take him in. His father was dead; his mother was locked up. No, other than Ten Bears, Logan had no one.

"I am alone in this world, your honor."

"Well, young man," the judge apologized, "budget cuts and societal indifference leave me little choice in this matter," he said, stamping some papers and then shuffling them from one pile to another.

"There's currently a one-year waiting list at every state-run orphanage in Colorado, so for the time being, we will have to make other...arrangements. Godspeed."

The judge's decision for a half-breed orphan with no family was painfully simple. Logan was shipped off to a juvenile detention center in Trinity to accept the harshest form of punishment he could imagine: the erasure of his Native American heritage and banishment from Raven and Ten Bears, the only two people he had left in this world.

Awakening from his dream, Logan rolled over and poked the fire in Radio's cabin, sending a trail of sparks up the chimney. It would be light soon, and he'd hardly slept a wink. As he gazed over at Raven sleeping peacefully, he hoped that one day he could reveal the burden that his troubled spirit carried to this day. Try as he might, it was a part of his past that he neither could change nor forget.

Chapter 07: Ten Bears

As the first light of morning streamed across the Continental Divide and into Radio's frosty cabin windows, Logan crawled out from under his sleeping bag and tossed a log on the smoldering fire. He rubbed his eyes and looked around; Radio was slumped over in his wheelchair, snoring like a lumberjack, and Raven was nowhere to be found. A static squawk crackled from the scanner. Radio startled, but then settled back into a restless sleep.

"You about ready, sleeping beauty?" Raven teased as she eased open the front door and pointed to her awaiting Percherons. "We're all saddled up and ready to go."

Logan thought about writing a note to let Radio know they were leaving, but decided not to interrupt his restful interlude.

"I'll be in touch," he whispered as he closed the door behind him.

It was a two-hour ride traversing the mountain trails to get to Ten Bears' sweat lodge, a path Logan hadn't traveled in many years. As they approached the small structure of aspen branches covered in elk skins, he studied the smoke rising from the lodge and remembered the last words Ten Bears had carved into his soul: *"It was a cold wind I felt on the mountain that day. The day your promise was broken and evil cast its shadow on this world."*

Raven dismounted and tied her horse to a tree by

the smoldering fire in front of the lodge.

Logan hesitated for a moment, then slid off his horse and handed the reins to Raven. He picked up a bundle of pale green foliage by the tepee and tossed it on the fire in front of the sweat lodge. As the dense grey smoke circled upward, he slowly waved it across his face, allowing the cleansing power of the sage to fill his lungs.

"Time to face the music."

Kneeling down, Logan peeled open the flap on the east side of the sweat lodge. Three paces inside the lodge was a buffalo skull on a post with a necklace of bear claws at its base. Across the darkened room he barely could make out Ten Bears, sitting motionless against the wall, cross-legged, his eyes closed. After a moment, the old man picked up a gourd and splashed water on the hot rocks in the center of the lodge, sending a wave of smoke and steam hissing into the air. He took a deep breath, waved an eagle feather, and sent a circle of vapors wafting toward Logan.

"Welcome back, Niwot," Ten Bears said as he slowly opened his eyes. "The time for healing has come. You and I have much to talk about."

Chapter 08: Sweat Lodge

Ten Bears sat motionless as the glow of red-hot stones in the center of the sweat lodge cast luminescent shadows across the elk skin ceiling. Logan knelt and took his place to the right along the wall, staring into the embers of the smoldering fire. After what seemed an eternal silence, Ten Bears spoke softly. "Raven has told me the truth of that day on Thunderbird Mountain."

"What did she tell you?"

"That it was her who first stumbled into the sacred cave of our ancestors ten years ago."

Logan hesitated, not wanting to relive his past. "We were playing…"

"Playing," Ten Bears smiled wryly. "And in your game, you looked upon the sacred drawings of the Ancient Ones."

"Yes, we saw the petroglyphs lining the walls."

"And you followed those drawings into the mountain?"

"We did," Logan confessed. "Only then did we realize that it was wrong, and we started to leave…but then I heard a growl from deep in the cave. Some kind of animal; it came from the darkness for us."

"What came for you in the darkness, few have ever seen. Fewer yet have lived to tell their story."

"What was it?"

"The Ancient Ones would say that you awakened an evil spirit in the cave that day."

"Whatever it was," Logan interrupted, "it locked onto Raven...and I...I tried to protect her. I got between her and the animal, I had my knife in my hand, but I don't remember much of anything else after that."

Ten Bears waited for Logan to gather his thoughts.

"Whatever it was," Logan continued, "it still haunts me in my dreams."

"I should think it would."

Ten Bears focused on Logan, studying his face and the way the smoke circled his body, lingering around his eyes and ears.

"Try harder. It is important. To remember that day, you must look into your mind's eye."

"I remember...There was a flash of light, and it was almost like a dream. I was floating in the clouds, flying on the back of a huge, strange bird. We were dancing in the air...until I felt a sharp pain in my chest. I couldn't breathe, and I gasped for air."

"Go on," Ten Bears leaned forward.

"I lost my grip and I slipped off of the bird's back. I was spinning, falling to Earth...almost to crash into a dark pool of water below." Logan tried to catch his breath. "The next thing I remember, I woke up here, in this lodge, with you."

Logan rubbed the scars on his throbbing ribcage and felt a chill run down his spine. "That's all I remember."

Ten Bears waited for Logan's breathing to return to normal before he spoke again. He reached inside the blanket by his side and pulled out a bloodstained seven-inch Marine KA-BAR and placed it into Logan's hand.

"My knife!" Logan gasped. "The one my father gave me. Where did you find it?"

"Where you left it, Niwot. That is enough for now.

When you open your mind, your memories will return."

Logan tried again to recover his memories of that day in the cave, but his mind was frozen in a recurring dream world, drifting in and out. There was a brief moment of panic. He could feel hot breath on his throat and a strange voice echoing in his mind, and he stabbed it with his knife. He felt another cold chill, terror, and the terrible pain. Then, there was only darkness.

Logan startled from his hallucination and opened his eyes. He was afraid to reveal any more of his recurrent dream to Ten Bears.

"No, there is nothing more, except…when I woke up here."

"That is all you remember?"

"No, I remember you were angry with me."

Ten Bears studied the beads of perspiration dripping down Logan's forehead, sensing that he was not fully revealing the memories of that fateful day in the cave.

"Yes, Niwot, I was angry with you. I mistakenly thought that you had violated my trust. I was wrong to have had so little faith in you."

Logan sat there silent in the sweat lodge, trying to calm his racing heart.

"You protected Raven from the evil in the darkness. For that, I am eternally grateful."

The steam from the rocks rose and filled the lodge, providing an impenetrable barrier to Ten Bears' quest for truth. Sensing that he had reached a temporary impasse, he redirected what seemed to Logan to be more of an inquiry than a reunion.

"Do you remember the first test of a Medicine Man?"

"I don't know," Logan mused nervously. "To not get killed?"

"You remember your lessons well," Ten Bears laughed. "That one, even I struggle with from time to time, so let us ponder the second test. It is to understand that the Spider of Heaven, the Creator, put each of us in this world for a special purpose. At first, his message may not be clear. His words may come to us in many forms: in nature, written in the stars, or sometimes a dream world, speaking truths that our inner ear is not yet ready to hear. To become a Medicine Man, you must open your mind to interpret the wisdom of his words, to hear what we are tasked to accomplish."

"I have tried to remember that lesson."

"Good. Our struggles in this world are intended to help us gain knowledge, and hopefully, ascend to a higher level. It may seem hard to understand, but it is only through our struggles that we can find understanding and fulfill our ultimate destiny. But our journey in this world is a perilous passage; it is as difficult to walk as a knife's edge."

Ten Bears' words of wisdom hung in the room, begging an answer from his reluctant student.

"If I were to rejoin you on the path to understanding, where would I start?"

"Your journey begins where your memory ends, so you must embark on a vision quest into the darkness of your spirit. Between the light and shadow, there you will find your understanding."

"But I don't know *how* to begin."

"You have returned to this lodge, Niwot. That was the first step in a journey that has already begun."

"So does that mean that…I'm your apprentice

again?"

Ten Bears poured another gourd of water on the fire and steam filled the lodge.

"Yes, you are welcomed back, on let us say, a trial basis. You still have much to learn, and to prove, Niwot…to me, and to yourself."

Logan gazed into the weatherworn face of Ten Bears across the sweat lodge, and in the corner of his eyes saw something he'd never seen before: fear.

"The darkness inside the mountain has awakened," Ten Bears stated flatly as he turned away. "And now its shadow walks among us."

Just as the words left Ten Bears' lips, the tent flap rustled, and Logan felt a cold wind on the back of his neck. Ten Bears reached inside the blanket by his side and gave Logan a small medicine bag filled with a tortoise shell, some herbs, and a feather.

"You will need this to resume your training. There is not much time."

"I have just one question," Logan hesitated. "Why me?"

Ten Bears raised his hand in a circle, pointing up at the ceiling of the sweat lodge. "The Wind Talker tells me that you are here for a reason," Ten Bears stated prophetically. "You have stared into the darkness of the mountain and looked upon the face of evil. The Ancient Ones whisper that few have seen through your eyes, and of those that have, most are dead. The ones that did not die…They ran away, trying to forget."

"I ran away. I tried to forget."

"You ran away, but you did not forget; it is inside of you. Something has called you back, to this time, to this place. The Wind Talker tells me this is so."

"But I don't know *why* I am here. I didn't choose

this place...this mountain," Logan said in a reluctant voice.

"No, you did not choose this mountain," Ten Bears said as he looked into Logan's troubled eyes. "This mountain has chosen you."

Chapter 09: Wind Talker

Logan peeled back the elk skin flap of the sweat lodge, shielded his eyes, and stepped into the glaring sunlight. Raven was waiting just outside with their horses saddled, anxiously scanning Logan's face for a reading on his homecoming with her grandfather.

Ten Bears emerged and hugged Raven.

"Thank you for bringing Niwot home," Ten Bears whispered.

"He's not comfortable with that name, Grandfather."

"I understand that," Ten Bears smiled. "But Lone Bear has been reborn in my eyes. He is now Niwot; one who has proven himself worthy of his ancestors. Had he lived, his father would have explained the significance of his heritage when he came of age. When I look into his eyes, I see his father in him, and he would be proud."

"Well, for now, he prefers to be called 'Logan.'"

Ten Bears turned and clasped arms with Logan, nodding his acceptance while ignoring her request.

"So, what did he think about Radio?" Raven blurted out.

"Oh, I almost forgot!" Logan exclaimed, pulling out his phone, "Guardian's message." He stepped between Ten Bears and Raven to replay the mysterious message that Radio had received in the ether.

"Sir, we've got another dead body," the garbled voice whispered on the police scanner. *"Well, at least part of one.* 40.3019246/ -106.9322714 / 2606. *Spirit Lake trailhead, ASAP."*

Ten Bears reflected in silence on the words he had just heard, then reached down and picked up a sage stick from the fire. He closed his eyes and waved the smoking sage three times over and below the phone before he spoke.

"I do not know what these words mean," he said, as he opened his eyes and turned to Logan. "But I suspect that they are the words of a Wind Talker. It is as I told you, the messages of the spirits may not always be clear, but they always reveal a truth."

"What do you think it means?" Logan asked.

"This truth was meant only for your ears. Open your mind, and it will come to you."

"Here's the only truth I know," Logan responded in frustration. "There's a delusional soldier with anger management issues holed up in a cabin on the mountain receiving weird messages on his scanner. The soldier contacts me to explain what it means, but I don't know what it means or even who the message is from!"

"Do not lose the meaning in the messenger. What is clear is, for some reason, this Wind Talker, 'Guardian,' you called her, has chosen your Radio for a special purpose. Through him, she has spoken to you."

"But *why* is she speaking to me?"

"The question is not why, but what. She gave you a trail to Spirit Lake, and knowing you, you followed it. What did you find at the end of the trail?"

Logan sat down on a stump by the fire and slowly recounted the horrific scene he'd discovered in the small clearing: the scattered remains of a man who had been ripped apart, strewn about, and partially consumed by what appeared to be a giant bear.

"It was more than just a bear," Logan whispered.

"I could feel that something dark and unnatural had been there." He closed his eyes and a cold chill ran down his spine.

"What do you see, Niwot? In your mind?"

"Something evil," Logan continued. Recounting the crime scene had dredged up that feeling, the feeling that he'd felt once before, long ago in the cave. When he opened his eyes, the strange feeling dissipated into the sunlight. It was gone.

Ten Bears sighed, reading the signs of apprehension written on Logan's face.

"It is as I feared," Ten Bears said as he turned away, staring into the burning embers of the fire. "The shadow now walks among us."

"What should we do, Grandfather?" Raven interrupted.

"Niwot must listen to Guardian; she will guide him," Ten Bears said softly. "A cold wind blows down from the mountain, and somehow, both her spirit and his are intertwined in this coming storm."

"How will I know what to do?" Logan asked.

"Follow the lessons you have learned: carry stones, make fire."

Raven shot a confused look to Logan.

Ten Bears put his hands on Logan's shoulders.

"Go down to the river, and find several large stones that part the waters. Carry those stones to the top of the mountain and place them in a fire ring. There, you must ask the Thunder Gods for their blessing."

"I have prayed to them before," Logan confessed, "but they never answered my prayers."

"Could it be because in your heart, you are not ready to believe?" Ten Bears asked as he studied

Logan's face. "Some men think that you must first see to believe. But a true Medicine Man knows that if the believing comes first, the seeing will follow. Believe, and then you will see."

"I will try," Logan responded.

"Trying will not be enough. The things I have told you, you must do. Everything you need to know is inside you. Remember my words and return to your vision quest, for it is there you will find your answers."

Chapter 10: Confessions

Hunched down in a giant, overstuffed leather chair at the Timberline Tea Haus, Logan stared at his laptop as the screen saver defaulted to a swirling Aurora Borealis dancing over the snow-covered peaks of the Rocky Mountains. Mesmerized by the pulsating beauty of pure energy, his mind drifted away from the din of his *Dark Talk* chat room bleating on in his headphones.

"You OK?" the waitress inquired as she nudged his shoulder.

Logan shook his head and was startled back to consciousness. "Yeah…I'm OK. Just a lot on my mind tonight," he said as he arranged the sugar packets on the table into a geometric pattern.

"Some complex computer gymnastics, I assume?"

"No, something more simple."

"Go on."

"I'm trying to understand…why I'm here."

"Hmm…herbal tea helps me clarify my thoughts," the waitress said as she poured a cup. "My own special blend tonight."

Logan wrapped his cold hands around the warm teacup and took a long drink. It had a bitter taste at first, then a sweet finish that seemed to dance on the back of his tongue. The aroma of the tea was familiar as well; he just couldn't place it.

"I'm lost," Logan began. "But I don't know where to start, really."

"Finish your tea, and I'm sure it will come to you."

Logan took a deep drink of the warm tea and relaxed his shoulders with a deep sigh.

"When you think about feeling lost," the waitress probed, "what's the first thing that comes to your mind?"

Logan smiled, took another drink, and closed his eyes. As he sank into the soft leather chair, he let his mind wander aloud. "Ten years ago, that's when I first got lost. The day I was forced to leave this mountain; that's when it started."

"Why did you leave the mountain?"

"I didn't want to leave, things just happened that I couldn't control. My dad was killed, and my mom broke down. Suddenly, I was alone and on my way to a juvenile detention center in the middle of nowhere."

"How did that make you feel?"

"Other than being lost, angry. I was angry at the world, but mostly I guess I was angry with myself."

"What happened?"

"I landed in the middle of a pretty bad situation down there in Trinity. My only friend there was this old Navajo janitor, Shay Niyol. Funny, he saw me sitting alone in the exercise yard one day and just started talking to me. We ended up talking on a regular basis, mostly him telling me stories about warriors and spirits, like my dad used to tell me. He had a workshop with a computer repair business he ran on the side, and he let me tinker around there any time I wanted. No other kid in the school even had access to a computer, so that was pretty cool. I finished high school online in his garage; all AP classes and some university credits. Not much of a social life, but it got me away from the Neanderthals in the yard, and I picked up some cash doing his service calls. One day, Shay sent me out on a computer repair call to the county coroner—said he was having data entry trouble. Turns out it was a user error I'd seen before; he was too drunk to type. So I logged in a few bodies, responded to some emails, and covered for him until he sobered up. He appreciated my discretion, so he slipped me twenty bucks and invited me back on a regular basis to help him with his 'data entry' issue—off the books, of course. It turned out to be a symbiotic relationship; I learned crime scene forensics, and he learned how to keep his afternoon benders concealed."

"And you liked that?"

"Yeah, besides the data entry work, talking with Shay got me thinking about something other than getting my ass kicked every day. He said understanding the old stories and my forensics hobby would help me forget about my anger. Said we half-breeds had to stick together."

"Half-breeds?"

"Yeah, turns out he was part Navajo, part Hopi. Didn't sit well with either side from his neck of the woods. Same as my mom being a Bahana."

"Did his stories help?"

"Yes. In a strange way, they did. But learning to focus my anger was what protected me."

"How so?"

"There were these bullies in school, a gang really. They started to rag on me because of my Indian name. Half-ass half-breed, they called me. Eventually, they moved to weaker targets because they thought I was crazy."

"They thought you were crazy?"

"Yeah, I did some irrational things to get them off my back, like talking backwards, but that's another story. They eventually left me alone, but there was this one kid, kind of sickly and feminine; they wailed on him relentlessly. After school one day, they stripped him naked and chased him into the woods. I was sitting alone when he stumbled on me. The bullies caught up to him; the kid was all bloody and crying, begging me for help. A voice in my head said, *Let him go, some people deserve what they get.*'"

"And did you?"

"I was going to, but when I saw the terror in that kid's eyes, something inside me just snapped. I stared down one of the bullies, and I could see he feared me. I didn't say anything, I just picked up a rock and beat him almost to death."

"Oh my gosh! What happened then?"

"Well, that weak kid was never picked on again, that's for sure, but I got expelled. *'No place here for a violent offender like you.'* So they kicked me to the curb. That's when the voice in my head said I should come back to this mountain, so I hitched a ride on a train headed north, and here I am."

Logan slowly opened his eyes and saw the waitress staring at him intently.

"Wow, I'm sorry I dumped all that on you."

"That's OK. Part of the job…It's what I'm here for."

The waitress smiled as she cleaned up the table with her apron. She started to leave but then turned back to Logan with an understanding look. "You know, everyone has a dark side, a primitive voice that tells us to strike back sometimes."

"I don't know what came over me. When I saw that pitiful kid who couldn't protect himself, it reminded me of…well, of me. I guess that was my trigger. I just reached a breaking point so I pounded that bully while the voice in my head was egging me on, louder and louder."

"What did the voice say?"

"It said, *Kill the bastard. Smash his brains out, he deserves it. End him.*"

"But you didn't."

"Kill him? No, I didn't…but I wanted to."

"In situations like that, sometimes our animal instincts take over. You know what they say, it's fight or flight."

"For me, it's more fight than flight these days."

"Maybe that's your defense mechanism, to protect yourself and others you care about."

"Maybe I'm the one that should have his brains bashed out. Or maybe, I'm just losing my mind. I could be crazy."

Logan looked the waitress in the eyes, searching her face for an answer until she looked away.

"Wait…are you telling me that you hear voices in your head, too?"

The waitress looked directly into Logan's eyes. "Sometimes, I do."

"And do you listen to them?"

"More than I should," the waitress admitted. "But I thought we were talking about you?"

"Yeah, OK, we were."

"Why did you change the subject?"

Logan looked away. "Because sometimes the voice tells me to do things…things I don't want to do."

After a moment of silence, the waitress leaned down and spoke softly into Logan's ear. "You don't have to do what the voice in your head tells you to do; you make your own decisions."

"Sometimes I don't think I do."

"Look, it's like when you saw that kid in need; you stepped in to help him. That was *your* choice. When you were punishing the bully, you could have killed him, but *you* didn't. You made those choices—the right choices."

"Yeah, a lot of good it did. As soon as I got thrown out of school, some other kid probably got his ass kicked the next day, and the day after that."

"Maybe, you can't save everyone. But maybe the kid you protected helped him fight back. Maybe all the kids that were getting picked on fought back because you stood up for the first one. Even a mighty river starts from a single raindrop."

"Unlikely," Logan sighed. "But I guess it's possible."

"Let's go back to where we started."

"Where we started?"

"Yes, you said you were lost and you came back to this mountain for a reason, a reason you are trying to understand."

"That's what really bothers me…I don't know why I'm here."

"Why are you here? Honestly? We've all wrestled with that question at one time or another. Give it some time, and you'll figure it out."

"But why did I come to *this* mountain?"

"I'm not sure, but two things seem clear to me: First, a man can only climb a mountain by taking one step at time. You're searching for the next step."

"And the second thing?"

"Somewhere out there, because of you, there's one less kid getting his ass kicked every day." The waitress smiled, touched Logan on the shoulder, and started to walk away.

Logan's impulse was to follow her, but the text translator on his computer interrupted their conversation. *"Truth Detector? Are you there?"*

Logan sat up in his leather chair, looked around at the empty room, and flipped open his computer. *'I'm listening,'* he messaged.

Chapter 11: Wapiti Meadows

High in his remote mountain cabin, Radio had been startled awake by the crackle of channel six of his police scanner. He flicked on his recorder and rolled across the room, rotating the frequency knob as he logged the garbled message.

2:07 AM, 25 degrees below zero.

"All right, all right, damn it!" he snapped, spilling his cup of tea. "I hear you!"

Powering up the antenna to his Internet satellite relay, he typed the message: *'Truth Detector? Are you there?'*

'I'm listening,' Logan typed back.

'Gunshots in the park.'

'What?'

'Another dead body.'

'Where?' Logan responded.

'Lovers Lane; Wapiti Meadows.'

'When?'

Radio stared at clock and the future time stamp on the message in his log, shaking his head.

'Soon.'

Chapter 12: Lovers Lane

The vibrating phone on the nightstand awakened Sheriff Martin's husband with a start, but not her; she'd never fallen asleep. Billie Sue rolled over, rubbed her eyes, and looked at the clock.

3:05 AM, 30 degrees below zero.

She pulled the pillow over her heard to try and mute the phone.

"Yeah?"

"Gunshots in the park, sir," the third shift police dispatcher announced.

"Again?" her husband moaned, pulling his covers over his head. "Tax season for the entire town, hello? Maybe you should sleep somewhere else!"

"Believe me, I've thought about that," Billie Sue barked back as she rolled out of bed and stumbled into the bathroom. She clicked on the overhead, looked in the mirror, grimaced, and turned off the light.

"If you woke me for some drunk elk hunters popping off a few rounds…"

"No, sir, not hunters. We've got another one."

"Another body?"

"Yes, sir."

"OK, OK. You didn't…?"

"Not unless you tell me to, sir."

"And have you called…?"

"He's already there, sir."

"Where?"

"Lovers Lane, up at Wapiti Meadows."

"Lovers Lane. That's sweet."

Chapter 13: Bear Vision

It was an eerie, moonlit night when Logan arrived in the National Park at Wapiti Meadows. Down a windy, dirt road that led to a clearing, he could make out the silhouette of a vehicle in the tall, dead grass above the snowfall.

"Hello?" he called out, hearing nothing in response but the echo of his voice and the hoot of an owl reverberating in the forest. A cold wind stirred through the trees, causing the hair on the back of his neck to bristle. He sniffed the air, closed his eyes, and his mind drifted into a dream state.

From the shadows of the tree line, a huge bear was watching. It turned its head, focusing its ears on the squeals and sudden shrieks of laughter coming from the clearing ahead. Moving slowly under the cover of the dead grass, it crept toward the human sounds wafting through the crisp night air. Ten feet from the vehicle, it sniffed the air, hunched down, and waited.

I choose you, the bear's thoughts echoed in Logan's mind.

Inside the old jeep, beads of moisture dripped down the steamy windows as the vehicle creaked and rocked back and forth. All of a sudden, the noise and motion inside the jeep stopped.

"Wait!" a girl's voice begged as she pushed the boy's hand from under her panties and sat up. "I heard something!"

The boy reached up and nuzzled his face into her

bare breasts, kissing them softly. "That's just your heart talking, baby," he mumbled. "Saying it wants me, now!" He slid his hand behind her thighs and pulled the girl down into the backseat.

The girl resisted for a moment and then relented, her face pressed against the glass of the foggy window. "You do love me, don't you?"

"Baby," the boy panted as he tugged the girl's jeans down around her knees and ran his hand up her inner thigh to a soft sigh of delight, "you know I…"

Tap, tap, tap. A sharp metallic sound on the window interrupted the lover's vows of infatuation.

"What the hell?" The boy sprang up from the backseat and wiped a small circle on the foggy window. "OK, OK!" he protested as he pulled up his pants and rolled down the window. "We're not doing anything wrong. What the hell do you…?"

Bang! Bang!

The gunshots echoed down the canyons of his mind as Logan was startled from his dream state.

Chapter 14: Crime Scene

Arriving at Lovers Lane, the headlights of Sheriff Billie Sue Martin's old pickup caught a lone figure standing by a Jeep station wagon in a clearing of tall grass.

How did he get here so fast?

The sheriff pushed open the creaky door of her pickup into the howling wind, zipped up her jacket, and crushed out a cigarette in the snow.

"OK, what do we have?" she asked as she approached Logan.

Logan scanned the old Jeep and slowly turned his head from the grass clearing to the trees, and then back to the sheriff.

"Couple of teens parking...boy in the Jeep's DOA—took one bullet between the eyes, one to the heart. Headshot's a through and through...broken glass on the passenger side where it exited the vehicle. From the angle, I'd say the bullet ended up in the snowbank over there. Second one's lodged in the rear door panel, mostly intact. Tracks leading toward the trees over there," he motioned. "But no sign of the girl."

Billie Sue shined her flashlight into the Jeep, taking note of the crime scene. A partially-clothed boy in the backseat, his shirt soaked in blood. Scattered on the floor were abandoned articles of the girl's clothing, and the driver's side rear door of the Jeep was almost ripped off the hinges.

"Doesn't look like a hunting accident," Sheriff Martin observed.

"Well, yes and no. It wasn't an accident, but it sure looks like hunting to me," Logan responded, pointing to the bear tracks and claw marks on the vehicle. "And he's no longer content with stealing a kill."

"This wildlife-related situation is quickly escalating," Billie Sue noted as she bent down to examine the large paw print in the snow.

"Don't step on that track," Logan cautioned.

"OK, why?"

"Never walk on an animal's trail, especially this one. Bad medicine, Sheriff."

"All right, that's good to know."

"Who do you think shot lover boy?"

"Definitely not Cupid's arrow," Billie Sue replied as she bent down and picked up a lace bra from the floorboard of the Jeep with a stick. "This guy used a gun."

As Logan and the sheriff examined the ground around the vehicle, a flickering light appeared in the tree line and advanced from the direction of the footprints leading away from the Jeep in the snow.

"I heard gunshots," the ranger called out as she approached the clearing. "This time of year, we get poachers up here at night. Didn't sound like a hunting rifle, so I called it in. What's the story, Sheriff?"

Billie Sue Martin studied the ground around the Jeep and then glanced over at the ranger. "Couple of shots, close range. One dead, one missing—and Yogi's back."

"You think the bear from the other night was involved in the shooting?" the ranger asked.

"Not unless he's packing," Sheriff Martin quipped, making a notation in her log.

The ranger peered into the Jeep at the dead boy in

the backseat and shook her head.

"Geez, you know how guys are these days," the ranger said, turning to Logan with a smile. "Always wanting to ride the bumper cars without a ticket."

"No means no," Logan shot back.

"I heard that," the sheriff chimed in, still studying the crime scene.

"Smells like teen spirit got a little out of control," the ranger volunteered, looking at the girl's clothing on the floorboard. "He says yes, she says no, and then bang! He's dead."

"Unlikely," Logan interrupted, facing the ranger. "She left her bra and one shoe in the car."

The ranger stepped back from the Jeep and Logan.

"Agreed," Billie Sue injected. "I'd say some guy shot the boy, then he went after the girl."

"What makes you think that?" the ranger asked.

"Two sets of tracks." Logan pointed to the snowbank by the Jeep, "Whoever killed the boy chased the girl toward the trees over there."

"Really? That's cold," the ranger said.

"Who would have done such a thing?" the sheriff asked.

"Any guy with a gun," the ranger injected. "The park's open carry now; that's the law."

"Looks like a nine millimeter," Logan added as he studied the exit wound on the back of the boy's head and then turned to the tracks leading to the woods. "Not a hunter or a plinker, I'd say, Sheriff."

"Nine millimeter?" the ranger questioned. "Sounds like some flatlander. A gangbanger, I bet."

"Powder burns on the boy's forehead," Logan observed. "No broken glass on the driver's side, just the passenger's side. The killer used a semi-automatic handgun; ejects forward and to the right, so the first shot came from outside the window. One shell casing beneath the front tire, second one on the floorboard. I'd say the killer reached inside for the shot to the heart, probably while the girl was scrambling around in the vehicle, trying to escape."

"That's hardcore. Anything else?" the sheriff asked.

"No sign of a struggle by the victim. The boy rolled the window down for the killer and took one between the eyes without a fight."

"Or his pants," the ranger sighed.

"So, our killer is calm and collected," Billie Sue outlined. "He walked right up on our lovebirds, had a chat, and then popped the boy."

"One more thing," Logan said. "There are no other tire marks around the Jeep. The killer was waiting out here in the cold, so he must know the park pretty well."

"OK, we're looking for a hardcore guy with a gun who knows his way around the park, traveling by foot," Billie Sue added. She turned to the ranger. "You seen anybody like that up here recently?"

The ranger paused for a moment and reflected before responding. "You know, now that you mention it, there was this one guy. Came in and bought a backcountry permit about a week ago. Sketchy dude: lip ring, tattoos, and attitude. Didn't say much, just paid in cash and left. You think we got ourselves an outlaw on the loose, Sheriff?"

"Maybe. It's worth checking out. Once we secure this crime scene, I'm going to need to see that permit."

"Sure thing. I'll send it to your office," the ranger nodded as she walked away.

"I've already called Search and Rescue," Logan said, as he cast his flashlight on the trail to the tree line.

"You know, in a perverse way, I hope she was taken by someone," Sheriff Martin lamented.

"Agreed. In this cold, she won't last long up here alone."

Billie Sue studied the tracks in the snow, walked around the Jeep once more, and looked inside at the girl's scattered clothing. She picked up the abandoned shoe from the backseat, dropped it in an evidence bag, and shook her head. "How are we going to find you, Cinderella?"

"We could have her try this on," Logan picked up the lace bra from the backseat with a stick and dangled it across his chest. "Just to see if it fits."

Before the sheriff could chastise Logan, her phone rang. "Hold on," she answered.

She glanced over at Logan, muted her phone, and signaled to him that their conversation for the moment was over. Stepping back into her old pickup, she closed the door and reflected on the crime scene. After a moment, she switched her phone off mute. "OK, it's secure."

The voice on the other end of the phone bleated on, and the sheriff closed her eyes, rubbing her forehead. "I know. I won't. He won't, not until I tell him to. Yes, I do know my job. I'm on the way."

Chapter 15: Town Council

Sheriff Martin pulled into the darkened parking lot of the Broken Axle Bar and Grill, waited for a couple of drunks to stagger down the street, and then slipped in the back door through the kitchen.

Inside, a young woman in a Deadhead T-shirt wiped down the bar, pulled the plug on the jukebox and nudged the last two drunks toward the exit. For locals and blue-collar rednecks, it was last call at the only lonely-hearts club in town open late in the dead of winter. The owner was having a drink in a dingy booth at the end of the bar, counting the night's receipts. Billie Sue glanced around the empty room and then slid into the booth behind him.

"What happened up at Wapiti Meadows?" the owner asked as he closed the cash box and pushed it aside.

"The council knows about that already? I haven't even filed my report."

"Nothing goes on in this town we don't know about."

"Yeah, everybody knows that. Here's what I've got so far: Two teens attacked on Lovers Lane, one dead boy, one missing girl."

"Any suspects?"

"I'm running down a backcountry camper from the flatlands. Looks to be some kind of outlaw; I like him for this."

"And the girl?"

"Search and Rescue's gearing up. They can't fly until dawn."

"You plugged in?"

"I've got eyes on the team."

"Listen to me. Find the girl or lose her, we don't care. Just get it done quietly. We don't want some missing cheerleader's face posted on every downtown street corner during the Winter Festival, you hear me?"

"I understand."

"One more thing, Sheriff. We keep our friends close and our enemies closer. Never confuse the two, and never make me doubt where you and me stand. Are we clear?"

"Crystal."

"Good, keep it that way. Any link to that other...accident?"

"I don't know yet, but I've got two dead bodies and bear tracks at both crime scenes."

The business owner exhaled a long breath, took the last drink of his whiskey, and slid closer to Billie Sue. "Look, Sheriff. It's a jungle out there; people die every day. Death, despair, and taxes... that's all there is. Most people get what they deserve in this life. That's the kind of crap that happens down the mountain; that's what's expected. But when tourists come up this mountain and get hung, shot by outlaws, and eaten by bears? That's not what's expected. That's bad, scary bad. Bad like some frickin' cheesy backwoods horror movie film festival, the one with scantily-clad coeds getting chewed up by chainsaws and tossed in the chipper. We don't want horror movies like that up here, do we, Sheriff?"

"No, we don't."

"We sure the hell don't! Look, this little wildlife

creep show you've got going is bad for business, so we bury the story along with the body; not because we want to, because they want us to. People come up here with their families to feel safe. They come up here to relax, breathe the fresh air, take a hike in the park, and then buy the kids a rubber tomahawk, a goofy 'I Took a Crap in the Woods' T-shirt and some week-old taffy. They come up here to leave their flatlander fears—and a good part of their wallets—behind…far behind. This is a safe, family-oriented frickin' mountain Shangri-La, not because somebody discovered it and planted a flag on it, it's because we *made* it, you got it?"

"I got it."

"Good, because we pay you and that pencil-neck taxman of yours to get it. And by the way, we're not going to cover his ass again, no matter who he's married to."

"And I appreciate it, sir. *We* appreciate it."

"You'd better."

"Is that all for tonight, Councilman?"

"No, there's one more thing, Sheriff. When you file that report of yours about the incident at Wapiti Meadows, the bear wasn't there, understand?"

"What do you mean?"

"You said a kid got shot?"

"Yes."

"Then it wasn't the bear, Sheriff. Bears don't use guns."

Chapter 16: Bear Killer

As Logan rounded the trail into a small clearing high in the mountains, he could see smoke swirling out of Ten Bears' sweat lodge of aspen branches. After cleansing his negative energy with smoke from the fire outside, he knelt down and entered the lodge of elk skins to find Ten Bears seated across the way, awaiting his arrival.

"Tell me, what have you learned, Niwot?"

Logan hesitated. The disturbing vision of the bear stalking the young couple at Wapiti Meadows still lingered in his mind. Before he could speak, Ten Bears interrupted his thoughts.

"I sense that the shadow that walks among us is getting stronger."

"Yes," Logan confessed. "It is; I can feel it."

"Describe the feeling."

"I feel that this shadow…somehow it's connected to the missing girl. She's lost on the mountain in the middle of winter. I have to find her before she's killed or freezes to death, but I can't find the trail."

"Embrace your vision. Sometimes it is what you do not see that is important. Travel in your mind back to the last place you felt the shadow."

Logan closed his eyes and visualized the crime scene at Wapiti Meadows. He was standing beside the car, following the girl's tracks to the tree line.

"There are…two sets of tracks," he said softly, turning his head as if to see. "But someone has dragged brush over the trail. Just before the tree line, I can see a track, a large bear track in the snow. The bear must have followed the girl to the edge of the trees. Then, they both disappeared." Logan opened his eyes. "How can a fifteen-hundred-pound bear disappear?"

"A bear that can disappear may not be a bear."

"Maybe it's not a bear," Logan exhaled. "Whatever it is, I think it has the girl."

Ten Bears waited for Logan to continue with his thoughts.

"My father taught me how to track a bear, and how to kill one. But if it is not a bear, how can I kill it?"

"If the bear you seek is not a bear," Ten Bears puffed on his pipe, "then to kill it, you cannot be a man."

"Now I really don't understand."

"It is not the bear that you seek," Ten Bears put down his pipe. "It is the shadow, Niwot. You must enter the Shadow World to kill it."

"I'm lost again," Logan sighed. "What is it that I am to do?"

"I will teach you what to do, when you are ready," Ten Bears said as he stirred the embers in the fire. "The Ancient Ones say that before you can defeat a shadow, the unknown, you must first see the world through its eyes. Only then will you know its weakness."

"But how would I do that?"

"To enter the Shadow World, you must enter a dream with your eyes open. You will learn to do this in time, but first, your mind must see through the eyes of others."

"OK…"

"In your mind, place yourself where others have been, study the surroundings carefully. Every branch, every footprint, every broken twig tells a story. Begin in your mind with what they saw, what they did, and what they thought."

Logan closed his eyes and envisaged the crime scenes at Spirit Lake and Wapiti Meadows. A sudden wave of alertness came over him as if he were there all over again. "I can see it now."

"Good. In your mind, first you will see *what* happened, then you will see *why* it happened. To do this, you must control your mind and see through the eyes of others. In your mind, you must become a part of them."

"I have imagined this many times in my dreams," Logan confessed, "but I didn't think it was real."

"It is real," Ten Bears smiled, sensing the progress with his apprentice.

"But you said you were going to teach me how to kill the bear."

"Patience, Niwot. Before you start down this path, you have much more to learn. To rush in before you are ready, it would end…badly. Part of your path is to understand the risks of the Shadow World, risks you must be prepared to accept."

"What risks?"

"For one, the risk that you may never return."

As Ten Bears' words hung in the air, Logan's mind drifted back into his past memories of the cave. In a blurry, chaotic moment, he again felt the sharp pain in his chest as he fell out of control, tumbling from the sky. This time, he plunged into a raging river and was swept over a waterfall, plummeting down into the icy cold darkness below. Many desperate, chaotic voices cried out to him, so agonizingly loud that he tried to cover his ears to stop the pain. They were spinning around him, all shrieking at once, and then a sudden cloud of hot steam in his face snapped him back to reality.

"Are you all right, Niwot?"

Logan took a deep breath and rubbed the aching scar on his chest. "I'm OK," he gasped.

"Then we must move quickly. As the shadow grows stronger, more death will come. Do what I have told you, and learn from the clues that are presented to you as you embrace your vision quest. Trust me, the answers you seek are there."

Logan tried to process Ten Bears' words, but one thought would not leave his mind: "If I do as you ask, will I learn fast enough to save the girl?"

"It does not matter," Ten Bears exhaled. "If you learn too slowly, she is dead anyway."

Chapter 17: Apprehension

Peering through the tangled brush alongside Wolf Creek in the Wild River Gorge backcountry, Logan spotted a lone figure next to a small tent, hunched around a portable camp stove. After tracking down the backcountry permit for the outlaw the ranger had described, a Search and Rescue helicopter had picked up the suspect's trail from where he was last seen in the park near eleven thousand feet, just below the timberline.

He's not getting away now, Logan thought, as he watched the suspect and remained deadly still.

"SR4," Logan whispered on his radio. "Beneath the cliff, just below Isolation Peak."

"Ten-four," Sheriff Billie Sue Martin acknowledged. "Deputies, move in…slowly!"

In moments, the remote campsite was surrounded, startling the outlaw. He stood up from the stove, took a long draw on his marijuana cigarette, and dropped the burning joint into a snowbank.

"You know the drill!" the sheriff shouted out. "Turn around, hands behind your back!"

"You run out of drunks to roll downtown, Marshal?" the outlaw taunted. "I ain't got no money for any of your trumped-up charges, so leave me the hell alone!"

As the sheriff was cuffing the man, the ranger scanned the campsite, picking up a backpack from his tent. She ruffled around inside the backpack and then zipped it back up.

"Hey, leave my shit alone!" the outlaw protested.

"You'll get your stuff back at the sheriff's office," the ranger replied, tossing it to a deputy, "Or when they let you out of the slammer."

"Incarceration? For what?"

"You're under arrest for murder," the sheriff interrupted. "The deputy will read you your rights."

"What are you talking about, Marshal? Can't a man enjoy some quite time alone in the mountains?"

"Quiet time, I can do, cowboy. I've got a jail cell for you that should just fit the bill. Let's go."

Chapter 18: Interrogation

Seated in the holding room of the Deadraven Sheriff's Department, Billie Sue Martin looked over a folder containing information on the man she'd just arrested in the backcountry of the Wild River Gorge. After a life of modest and mostly random crimes, it seemed the man lately had become a more focused and violent criminal. He'd served time for some of his recent offenses: vandalism, arson, a shooting, and a suspected bombing. Oddly, he'd secured early release from prison after intensive pressure from the attorneys of a wildlife animal rights lobby group known to be affiliated with eco-terrorism.

"You've got quite a sheet here," Billie Sue began. "What's your problem?"

"My parents didn't love me," the outlaw said smugly. "Just a cry for help, you know."

"Did the boy you shot cry for help?"

"Hey, if some kid got popped, I don't know nothing about that."

"Yeah, we'll see about that. Says here you just got out of Trinity two weeks ago. What are you doing all the way up here, anyway?"

"I've paid my debt to society, Marshal. When I dumped my peels, I needed a change of scenery, so I came up this way to enjoy the peace and quiet of the wilderness, you know? A Rocky Mountain holiday...saw it on a travel brochure in the joint—looked nice. Thought I'd get back to nature, do some camping. The 'call of the wild' so to speak."

"Why'd you need a gun to go camping?"

"I don't have a gun, Marshal. You know it would be illegal for a convicted felon like myself to possess a firearm."

"Well, we found this nine millimeter Glock in your backpack," the sheriff barked as she tossed the semiautomatic pistol in a plastic bag onto the table.

The outlaw looked at the gun and shrugged. "Never seen that before, man."

"You've got a rap sheet as long as my arm," the sheriff said as she glanced down at the folder in front of her. "And it looks like your last little adventure at that construction site you torched? You shot a security guard...with a nine millimeter. What a coincidence."

"I told you, that gun ain't mine, man."

"We're running your prints right now. I'm betting this is the gun you used to shoot my kid up in the park. Come clean now, and maybe we can work something out."

"I told you, I didn't do no kid! Not my style, man. Besides, everybody knows that it's bad juju to do a kid. I'd be dancing on the blacktop first time I hit the yard at Trinity."

"Dancing?"

"Yeah, man, shanked, stabbed on the exercise yard with a makeshift knife. Dead. Dudes in there won't tolerate a kid-killer on the block."

The door opened and a deputy stepped in to hand the sheriff a forensics report. Sheriff Martin looked over the report and then glanced back at the deputy in disappointment. There were no fingerprints on the gun; it had been wiped clean.

Before the sheriff could speak, a well-dressed

young woman carrying a briefcase pushed her way into the room and wedged herself between her and the outlaw.

"Don't say anything more," she commanded. "I'll handle this."

The young woman slammed her briefcase down on the table and faced the sheriff.

"You've got a weapon here, alleged to have been used in a murder. Is that right, Sheriff?"

"We do, Counselor."

"Did you find my client's fingerprints on the alleged murder weapon?"

"No, not exactly. The gun had been wiped clean."

"Did you recover any DNA evidence that puts my client at your crime scene?"

"We're working on that. We took his sample, but we have to send DNA and ballistics out to a lab in the valley. We don't have that kind of equipment here."

"Do you have any witnesses that can place my client at your crime scene, Sheriff?"

"No, at least none that are currently alive. But as soon as we locate the girl…"

"So you have no witnesses, no murder weapon, and no forensic evidence that my client was even at your crime scene."

"I told you, we're working on that. We don't have the equipment…"

"Then we're done here, Sheriff. Release my client immediately, or we'll sue you and everyone in this one-horse town for false imprisonment and whatever else we can dig up. Judging by the quality of your detective work, I'm betting we'll bury you."

The outlaw stood and smiled as he started toward the door. The sheriff signaled the deputy to block the exit.

"I'm afraid I'm going to have to hold your client for a bit," the sheriff insisted.

"On what charge?" the lawyer demanded.

"Smoking in the park."

"Wake up, hayseed!" the outlaw blurted out. "Read the frickin' papers, man! It's legal to smoke pot in Colorado!"

"Pot's legal, smoking isn't," the sheriff stated bluntly. "It's against the law to have an open fire in the park—any fire. Wildfire danger, you know. Really bad for the animals." Billie Sue smiled at the lawyer.

"You've got to be kidding," the lawyer exclaimed.

"Oh no, I'm quite serious, Counselor."

The sheriff got in the outlaw's face and grinned.

"Like Smokey says, 'Only you can prevent forest fires.' Twenty-four hours, hayseed."

Chapter 19: Another One

"All right, damn it!" Radio snapped as he moved across the room in his remote cabin to the crackle of his cellular monitors. Screeching voices, text messages, and then cell phone calls, all talking over each other. "What the hell is this babble?"

6:35 AM, 5 degrees.

As he powered up his Internet satellite to record the garbled parts of the messages he could lock on to, the lights in the cabin flickered on and off as his wall of sophisticated equipment faded to silence.

"Shit! Not now!" Radio cursed as he rolled over to the wall and kicked the generator cables. He ripped the back panel off the smoking power relay and sighed. Every fuse was blown; this would take an hour to fix.

Working as fast as possible, he carefully rewired the fuse box and slammed it shut. Finally, with the equipment repaired, he again attempted to reach Logan. *'Truth Detector? I think we've got another one.'*

"Really?" Logan mumbled, roused from his sleep. He'd closed his eyes for what seemed like a moment before being startled awake again on the sofa of Cody Winston's garage. Logan's mind had been swirling through the vivid dreams, primitive instincts and blurry thoughts of an animal scavenging for food. However, this time the visions of Logan's dream world left him with something different: a putrid smell on his pillow.

"OK, Radio," Logan clicked on his microphone and shook the cobwebs from his head. "I'm listening."

"Something weird on my cellular frequencies, man."

"What is it?"

"Garbled voices, people screaming, like sheer panic..."

"What do you think is it?"

"Sounds like tourists from the accents, and horses, I think," Radio responded.

"OK, anything else?"

"Yeah. Gunfire and a dead body."

"Where?" Logan rubbed his eyes, still trying to awaken from his dream.

"The landfill over behind Wuutaqa Mountain."

"When?"

"I recorded the mayhem at 6:35 AM, but the cell time stamp was an hour later. Tried to get to you sooner, but my generator blew. I tried, man."

There was only static for a moment, and then Radio resumed the exchange. "Truth Detector? Are you there?" Radio pleaded.

"Yes, sorry." Logan shook his head. "I'm still trying to wake up. Look, you did what you could. I'll call it in and get over there to check it out."

"Logan?" Radio said softly.

"I'm listening..."

"Can't you make her stop? I don't want to hear this anymore."

"I'm working on it, Radio. We all want it to stop."

Chapter 20: Breakfast Ride

"Breakfast burrito and a cup of Joe, black and leaded," Billie Sue Martin shouted into the clown's face as she lowered her window in the drive-through lane.

"No doughnuts this morning, Sheriff?" the clown laughed. "We've got fresh sprinkles."

"Watching my weight, Bozo. Make it pronto on the caffeine."

Before Sheriff Martin could down the first gulp of coffee for the day, her police radio squawked good morning.

"Sir, we got another one!" the dispatcher interrupted.

"Really? Before breakfast?"

"Afraid so, we've got a..."

"Don't you say it while I'm eating!"

"No, sir, I won't."

"Thank you."

"Sir, we've got...someone who's not currently alive, sir."

"OK." Billie Sue took a bite of her burrito and burned her mouth. "Hot, damn it! Where?"

"The landfill, behind Wuutaqa Mountain."

"Can it at least wait until I at least have a cup of coffee?"

"No, sir, I don't think so."

"Why?"

"Shots fired, sir."

"Gunfire before breakfast?" Sheriff Martin exclaimed, as she spilled her coffee and dropped what was left of the burrito on her shirt.

"Crap! That's not coming out," she cursed under her breath, attempting to wipe the burrito residue up with her tie. "OK, did you log this one yet?"

"Just the shots fired, sir."

"All right. That's good."

"I didn't log the part about the person who's...who's not currently alive, sir."

"Outstanding. You call him?"

"No, sir."

"Why not?"

"He called me."

Chapter 21: Dumpster Dive

Arriving at the riding trail on Wuutaqa Mountain above the landfill, the sheriff approached Logan as he was questioning two wranglers from the Moosehorn Lodge and Guest Ranch.

"Someday, you and me need to talk about how you get to these crime scenes ahead of me," the sheriff demanded as she rubbed the stain on her uniform, smearing it even more. "And how you find your clues."

Logan glanced at her, and then down at her shirt. "We've got a real problem here, Sheriff."

"Really?" Billie Sue leaned in closer.

"Burrito stain. That's not coming out."

"Tell me about it," Billie Sue wrinkled her nose as she stepped back from Logan, reacting to his foul odor.

"Sorry, didn't have time to change."

"OK, what do we have?"

"Wranglers from the Moosehorn were leading their sunrise ride up Wuutaqa Mountain, past the landfill. One of the tourists spotted an animal on the landfill, so the wranglers herded the group closer for a snapshot."

"That's special," Billie Sue said sarcastically.

"It was special, until one of the guests noticed it was a huge bear on the trash pile, and it had something unusual in his mouth."

"Which was…?"

"A human arm."

"That could cause you to blow your groceries."

"It did, for several of the guests."

"Now that was a Kodak moment."

"Yeah, that's when all hell broke loose."

"What about the gunfire?"

"Turns out it was just blanks. One of the wranglers was chasing the bear away; she's one of those cowgirl mounted shooters."

"Nice. Caught that show at the fairgrounds last year, quite entertaining. Long Colts popping balloons and such; those girls put on quite a show."

"I like the mutton bustin' myself."

"Kids riding sheep, it never gets old, does it? Back to our gun-toting cowgirl; what happened?"

"Seems she was afraid the bear might turn on the Midwest paparazzi and spook the dude horses. Said she was just trying to head off having a load of greenhorns ditched all over the mountain."

"I hear that," the sheriff said as she scanned the group of harried tourists down by the barn. "What about the body?"

"Male, middle-aged, over in the landfill. I covered him up; not much left for identification. Looks like our bear started munching on him a while back and returned this morning to finish off his meal. Once a bear gets the taste for human flesh, we're just the other white meat."

"That's what I was afraid of. We've got a man-eater, all right."

"Probably don't want that on the travel brochure."

"I'm thinking not. Nothing else we can do here until we get the coroner's report," Sheriff Martin pronounced as she strung yellow police tape around the dumpster. "Where are we on the missing girl?"

"Nowhere," Logan sighed. "I've been over the trail

at Wapiti Meadows three times; not a trace of the girl after her tracks leave the clearing. Deputies checked with her folks; she never came home last night."

"Twelve hours. If we don't find her by tonight…"

"I know, we'll never find her."

Chapter 22: Outlaw

The phone rang at the Deadraven Sheriff's Department, echoing down an empty hallway; it was the coroner with his report on the half-eaten body from the landfill.

"You're on speaker, Frank," Billie Sue quipped. "Tell me something good."

"This one took me a while," the coroner started. "Not much to work with."

"That's why you make the big bucks and get all the ladies."

"Funny. I was able to reassemble most of your John Doe's skull from the fragments."

"Go on…"

"It's not what you'd think at first glance. I'd say the cause of death was a gunshot wound to the head."

"What?" Sheriff Martin sat up in her chair.

"Close range, back of the head."

"All right…what caliber?"

"Hard to say, but definitely a handgun. Could be a nine millimeter, but I don't have a bullet."

"Well, that's not going to help me much. Wait, what about the bear? The man-eater?"

"Good news on that one. This guy was dead before the bear got to him."

"Poor son of a bitch. Shot and then eaten…several times."

"That's the order I'd pick if I had a choice."

"Have to agree on that one, Frank. What about the

time of death?"

"Now that's the interesting part, Sheriff. Quite a while ago."

"Can you be more specific?"

"No, I really can't."

"Why don't you take a guess?"

"OK, I'd guess...at least three weeks."

Sheriff Martin scratched her head and looked out the window.

"What do you make of this one, Frank? The trash around here gets picked up from town dumpsters once a week and trucked to the landfill, just like clockwork. Someone who had a rancid body decomposing in his dumpster would have noticed the smell before now, don't you think?"

"Not really."

"Why would that be?"

"Because the body wasn't decomposing; it was embalmed. Well, part of it, at least. The parts that people see, the face, neck, and hands, they're all embalmed. The rest of the body, not so much."

The sheriff leaned back in her chair, thinking, spun around, and looked out the window again.

"You haven't shared your findings with anyone else, have you, Frank?"

"No one but you...oh, and that attractive young lawyer that stopped by this morning. She brought doughnuts, the ones with the little sprinkles. Fresh ones, too, not like the stale bear claws you always bring. Said she was working on a case with you."

Just then, the door to the sheriff's office swung open. The outlaw's attorney pushed her way past a deputy and got right up in Billie Sue's face. "Your twenty-four hours are up, Sheriff," the lawyer commanded. "And don't even bother trying to link my client with your three-week-old bear attraction at the landfill. I already checked with your good buddy Frank at the coroner's office on this one. My client wasn't released from Trinity until two weeks ago, so go find some other innocent drifter to hang that one on."

The sheriff started to protest but then backed down and nodded to the deputy to clear the doorway.

"All right, I'll release your client for now," Billie Sue relented. "But don't let him leave town; he's still a suspect in a murder investigation. I may have some more questions for him."

"Oh, we'll stay in town for a while longer...long enough to file a lawsuit against you, Sheriff."

"County clerk's office is down the hall. Get in line."

Sheriff Billie Sue Martin closed her eyes and rubbed her forehead. She was puzzled. *Three dead bodies, a missing girl, no suspects, a man-eating bear on the loose...and now back to square one.*

Seated just outside the sheriff's office, Logan had eavesdropped on the entire conversation with the coroner and the heated exchange with the outlaw's lawyer. He walked in and plopped down on a sofa across the room.

"Who the hell shoots a guy," Billie Sue wondered aloud, "embalms the body, and then dumps it in the trash?"

"A three-part question...OK, I'll play. Who shoots a guy?" Logan answered. "First off, I don't have a clue. Move on to the second question first."

"You mean, who embalms a guy?" the sheriff followed.

"There's only one guy up there that does

embalming," the coroner interrupted, still on the speakerphone.

"Damn it, Frank! You been on there the whole time?" Sheriff Martin quipped.

"Yep!" the coroner cackled.

"And you let me take that beat down? Some friend you are."

"We reap what we sow, Sheriff. But I digress. There's only one embalmer up your way, to my knowledge."

"And that would be?" Logan asked.

"One Henry Hyde, your friendly neighborhood funeral director."

The sheriff jumped up from her chair and barked down the hall: "Get me anything we have on this Mr. Hyde. In the conference room, people! Now!"

Chapter 23: Mr. Hyde

The sheriff taped up a picture of funeral director Henry Hyde on a hastily assembled murder board in the conference room. Across the room, Logan was scouring multiple computer screens of incoming information, building a profile of their new suspect.

"What do we know about Mr. Hyde?" the sheriff asked.

"He owns a gun," one deputy responded, panning through background checks online. "And he has a concealed handgun permit. Also, looks like he logs time at the indoor range every week, just like clockwork."

"Caliber?" the sheriff asked.

"Nine millimeter, mostly. Buys his ammo at the range. He's a hiker; he's got a backcountry permit and a park pass."

"Interesting…"

"Here's something else," Logan interrupted. "This guy's a doctor, or at least he was one. It appears he lost his license to practice medicine. Let's see why…"

"I'm liking this guy." The sheriff hunched down behind Logan's screen.

"There were charges filed at his hospital," Logan read aloud.

"What charges?"

"Allegations that he groped a teenage girl in the emergency room."

"Details?"

"The report is mostly a 'he said, she said,'" Logan

continued. "He denied it, but her boyfriend backed up the charges. Wait, actually, the boyfriend *filed* the charges."

"Conviction?" the sheriff wheeled around.

"Never went to trial," a deputy who was scanning court documents answered from across the room. "It was settled; looks like the hospital paid out a boatload of hush money."

"Terms?"

"None. It's sealed with a nondisclosure. But the hospital board fired Dr. Hyde anyway; that's when he lost his medical license."

"Anything else?" the sheriff inquired.

"Yes," Logan said slowly. "I'm looking at the complaint filing. It's been redacted, but here's a log entry. His accusers were…the dead boy and missing girl from Wapiti Meadows!"

The sheriff turned around and grinned at Henry Hyde's picture on the murder board.

"There's our motive: A disgruntled doctor wants to settle the score with his teenage troublemakers."

"And opportunity: A backcountry hiker with a gun that fits," the deputy added. "A nine millimeter."

"Hold on," Logan interrupted. "Remember our first victim up at Spirit Lake, Dr. Malcolm Kennedy? I'm scanning the corporate filings. It says here that Dr. Kennedy was the head of the same hospital board that fired our Mr. Hyde."

"Well now, this just gets curiouser and curiouser," Billie Sue wrinkled up her brow.

The sheriff removed her firearm, checked the magazine, and then slammed it back in the holster.

"I think our Dr. Hyde may have a bit of Mister Jekyll in him," Sheriff Martin pronounced. "Deputy?

Why don't you go pay our friendly neighborhood funeral director a visit?"

Chapter 24: Epiphany

Upon arriving at the local funeral parlor, the sheriff's deputy radioed that Mr. Hyde had left work early, as it seemed was his usual practice on Wednesday afternoons. The receptionist suggested that he could be located at his "other office"—a bar downtown. Light snow just was starting to fall again, making crosstown travel slower than usual for Sheriff Martin and Logan.

"It all seems to fit, but something still doesn't seem right about this guy," Logan wondered aloud.

"It never does," Sheriff Martin countered. "One thing I've learned in all my years of detective work is that sometimes you just get lucky. Now that we can see the whole picture with this scumbag, all the pieces fall neatly into place."

"What is not seen is as important as what is seen," Logan thought, recounting Ten Bears' words. "OK, the revenge angle, I get that," Logan proffered. "But why seek your revenge up here in the mountains where you live? And why now?"

"They say that revenge is a dish best served cold. I'd say the frosty temperature of this crime spree fits that bill."

"Maybe, but wouldn't it have been easier for Dr. Hyde to seek his revenge down in the valley?"

"You'd think so, but criminals don't always stick to a well thought-out plan. They see an opportunity, something snaps, and bang! We've got another dead body."

"I'm just thinking, other than revenge, what else do our three dead bodies have in common?"

"The bear buffet?" the sheriff laughed.

"What if that had something to do with the killings?"

"The bear?"

"Yes, the bear."

"OK, I'll bite. This place is crawling with bears, especially near the landfill. With winter setting in, it's their last chance to fatten up before hibernation. Where are you going with this?"

"I don't know, but this bear seems to be tied in somehow. And black bears hibernate in late fall, not winter. Why isn't our bear asleep?"

"I don't follow…bears are omnivores, they'll eat anything. There's plenty of food in this town for the taking; just look in any dumpster."

"But what if this bear wasn't?"

"Wasn't what?"

"An omnivore."

"Well, I guess he'd be a carnivore then—a meat eater."

"What kind of bear only eats meat?"

"Some grizzlies, and polar bears, but no bear from around here," the sheriff started to follow Logan's line of thinking. "You know, you're right. All we have around here are black bears; the last grizzly in Colorado was killed back in the seventies."

"So there are no grizzly bears in Colorado?"

"No, there's been talk of reintroducing grizzlies in the mountains, but like the wolves, the park service says they can't manage another apex predator."

"Well, this bear eats meat, human meat. That makes it a man-eater."

The sheriff wheeled into a parking space in front of the Broken Axle, checked her firearm, and put her hand on Logan's shoulder.

"Listen, if your man-eater theory were true, we'd have a whole different problem," the sheriff reluctantly agreed. "I don't even want to go there. Hold that thought, we've got a murderer to collar."

The smell of stale beer and one too many happy hours greeted them as they walked into the bar.

"So this is the funeral director's 'other office'?" Logan observed.

Sheriff Martin scanned the patrons parked at the bar and the game room for her suspect.

"It's not so strange; a big-city doctor loses his license and gets exiled in disgrace to this backcountry town. He's reduced from a life of privilege to painting happy faces on old mangled dead bodies for the rest of his sorry life. Lipstick on a pig, that's all he's got left to look forward to."

"Don't forget he's a registered sex offender," Logan added, "part of the settlement. That might make him a tad unpopular at the local watering holes if the word got out."

"Yeah, that was probably the last straw. He slinks in here, parks himself on a bar stool, and drowns his troubles to wash away his past. Where the hell else would he be?"

"You're right. Redemption, happy hour, and chicken wings. This would be my office if I was him."

Chapter 25: Home Office

Sheriff Martin and Logan pushed their way through the crowd into the game room of the Broken Axle Bar and spotted Henry Hyde slamming away at the sides of a pinball machine. His quarters spent, the former doctor positioned himself snuggly behind a young girl dropping change into a machine to offer her his...assistance.

Billie Sue wedged herself between the game patrons, opening her jacket just enough to reveal her badge to both of them.

"Sorry to interrupt your game," the sheriff said as she turned to the girl, "but I've got a few questions for the pinball wizard here. It's about a dead body."

The girl shot a glance to her new partner, collected her purse, and walked away quickly.

"Thanks for that," the funeral director said as he swigged his beer and winked at the quickly departing teenager. "I've always appreciated the indiscretion of Deadraven's finest." Henry Hyde's smile quickly faded as he turned to the sheriff. "What is it, Sheriff? Running low on your parking ticket quota today?"

"No, but I'll be happy to check your meter when we leave."

"Fine, if I owe a quarter, put it on my tab."

"Actually, Mr. Hyde, I'm here for another reason. We found a dead body this morning in a dumpster out by Wuutaqa Mountain."

"What do you want from me? A finder's fee?"

"Look, Doc," Billie Sue lowered her voice and stepped closer. "I've actually got a couple of dead bodies, and I think you may be involved somehow."

"Oh, I get it. Any time you've got a problem, it's time to round up the usual suspects. Me, the town drunk, and that guy that won't admit he's stopped beating his wife. He never did, you know."

"I know about your past," the sheriff continued.

"Yeah, so does everyone else in this town with an Internet connection."

"You had some trouble with a young girl down in the valley, so I think you came up here to hide from your past. You tried to forget about ruining your life, but you couldn't let it go, could you?"

"Cut to the chase, Sheriff. Cast your aspersions, file your reports, and slap me with your bogus parking ticket. Just do what you have to do and leave me alone. It's my afternoon off."

"The body we found in the dumpster had been embalmed," the sheriff continued, looking for a reaction from the funeral director.

"So?"

"So, from what I hear, you're the only guy in this neck of the woods that's into that game."

"You know, I'm getting really tired of being every dip-shit detective's scapegoat. Duh? You can buy the chemicals for embalming at any feed store. Why don't you go round up all the farmers in the county and shake them down? I'm sure more than one of them has a few skeletons in his closet. You might even find Farmer John's grandma chained up in his basement; she's been missing for years, so I heard."

"He's right," Logan interrupted. "About the chemicals; they're actually pretty common."

The sheriff's phone rang, interrupting her questioning of the funeral director. "All right, OK," she responded, obviously irritated. "Now…Yes, I understand."

Billie Sue turned back to the former doctor. "We need to continue this discussion down at the station."

"You arresting me?"

"No, but I will if you don't stop by to visit— voluntarily, that is."

"I know your type, Sheriff. You'd arrest me right now if you had anything. You've got nothing but a fishing expedition, and I'm not biting."

"Oh, I don't know. I'll come up with something. Like you said, someone's grandma's always missing."

Henry Hyde paused and finished his beer. He pulled out his phone and dialed, smiling at the sheriff.

"By the way, you can forget about my vote in the next election."

"I can live with that."

"Hold on…my lawyer wants to know if you have an extra pair of pants at your office?"

"Why's that?"

"Because we're going to sue yours off."

"Get in line at the county clerk's office, Doc. Put it on my tab."

Chapter 26: We Like Money

Watching the sheriff questioning Henry Hyde from a remote video monitor in his private office, the owner of the Broken Axle Bar lit up a cigar and switched off the display; he'd seen enough.

The sheriff's phone rang, interrupting her questioning of the funeral director.

"Tell me that you have our man, Sheriff," the council member asked. "Henry Hyde, never trusted him, too much baggage. We want this matter put to bed, immediately."

"All right, OK," the sheriff responded, obviously irritated.

"In my office, now. Use the back door."

"Now...Yes, I understand."

After walking outside with Logan, the sheriff stopped abruptly, tossing him the keys to her truck.

"I'll meet you back at the station in thirty minutes," she grumbled. "I've got something to take care of."

Logan paused, noticing that the sheriff seemed particularly disturbed by the phone call she'd just received. "Anything I can do?"

"On this? No. Just get everything we have on Dr. Jekyll and meet me in the holding room."

"Ten-four."

The sheriff saw the confusion on Logan's face and felt an explanation was needed, at least enough of an explanation to keep him focused on locating the kidnapped girl. "It'll be dark soon," Billie Sue offered. "If we don't crack this guy soon, the chances of finding our missing girl in the mountains slips away. Find me a clue, something we missed, anything to hammer this bastard with. I'll be there directly."

As soon as Logan pulled out of sight, Sheriff Martin ducked down the alley and in the back entrance, making her way to the upstairs office of the Broken Axle Bar. The town councilman was seated behind a giant oak desk watching a wall of video surveillance screens from all over the town. He tapped his cigar on an ashtray as he swiveled his chair around.

"Is this Hyde our guy?" he asked, blowing a puff of smoke in the sheriff's direction.

"I think so."

"Sorry bastard. What do you have on him?"

"He got caught up in a sexual predator case with two kids in the valley. Settled out of court, but it cost him his job. It looks to me like he tracked his teenage accusers up here and decided to settle the score in Wapiti Meadows. He may be involved in another killing, but I'm focused on the missing girl right now. It's dicey, but she may still be alive."

"Make him sweat," the councilman grunted. "And get a signed confession. We want this situation under control, and fast."

"I'm working on it."

"With the drought, wildfires, and floods, bookings are down fifty percent for the season already," the councilman opined as he looked out the window at passing tourists. "Shangri-La doesn't need any more bad publicity, understand?"

"I understand."

"This incident at the landfill, another bear

situation?"

"Looks that way."

"Keep the bear out of this. That's an order."

"I know how to do my job, Councilman. I'm an elected official, you know."

The councilman chomped down on his cigar, crushed it out, and stood facing the sheriff, scanning her from head to toe. "Yeah, you're an elected official," the councilman smiled, "but we're the ones that got you elected, and we're the ones who can get you *un*elected anytime we want to."

"Need I remind you that…"

"Don't go playing your genealogy card, because that dog won't hunt anymore. You abandoned your ancestry to become a big-city detective down in Austin, but when you crossed the line and needed some dirty work, you called us, didn't you? If our cleaner hadn't taken out the trash, you and that pencil-neck would be pushing up bluebonnets in the Hill Country about now. So, we don't need to be reminded of anything, Sheriff. The way we see it, we're holding the deck, and you'll play the hand that's dealt you. We'd rather you just say thank you, and get back to the job we brought you here to do. You do remember what that job is, don't you?"

"Yes, sir, I remember."

"You're an elected official? Big frickin' deal. We could get an elk elected mayor in this town if we wanted to. You know what, that's not such a bad idea. May I present to you the honorable mayor of Deadraven: Ernie the Elk. We could plaster his rack on Burma-Shave billboards from Topeka to Trail Ridge. Think of the marketing, the publicity, the merchandising…Why, every ankle biter from the valley would beg to buy his very own Ernie doll. I'm writing that one down."

The hair on Billie Sue Martin's neck started to bristle; she could swallow naked commercialism, but threatening her family, that stuck in her craw. She started to fire back, but then caught her tongue at the last moment, taking a cleansing breath.

"Look, I'll nail this lowlife."

"And just how do you plan on doing that, Sheriff?"

"Guys like him make mistakes; they devolve. They get jacked up on their mission, they get sloppy, and they leave clues. I'll crack him and put this story to rest so your entire council can get their panties out of a knot."

"Careful, Sheriff. You might want to reassess the boundaries of your own panties."

"And what's with this bear protection paranoia anyway? You want me to do my job, then tell me what's going on around here, will you?"

The councilman turned away, plopped down in his leather chair, and lit up another cigar. "It's simple," he said, taking a puff. "Bears bring tourists; tourists bring money. We like money."

"I've got three dead bodies, and all you care about is *money*?"

"Don't be naïve, Sheriff. It's always about money."

"That's disappointing."

"Who do you think pays the bills in this town? It's not the ice cream eating tourists who ask, 'Where do you keep the Elk at night?' Or, 'When do the Elk turn into deer?' No, it's those damn bears that pay the bills in this town, that's who."

"OK, I get it."

"I don't think you do, Sheriff. Who pays your more-than-generous salary? Who keeps that pencil-pushing nimrod of yours gainfully employed beyond his meager mathematical abilities? The bears do. Really, for everything those bears bring to the party, I think they ask very little."

The councilman stood and looked out the window again at the shoppers overloaded with packages as they meandered from store to store on Main Street.

"Make my bear problem go away, Sheriff. Make it go away so we can all get back to business, the business of making money. Money, for *all* of us."

"OK, I get it. I've got a people problem, not a bear problem."

"Go put a killer in jail, Sheriff. Now you've got your head screwed on right."

"Screwed indeed. Anything else?"

"Yeah, never pass on an opportunity to keep your mouth shut."

Chapter 27: Vision Quest

Dead bodies, kidnappers, and a man-eater…

Before regrouping with Sheriff Martin, Logan decided maybe it was time to step back and look at the current crime spree with a set of fresh eyes—maybe several. He climbed the mountain, purified his thoughts, and entered the sweat lodge, seeking the counsel of Ten Bears.

"I'm at a dead end," Logan began. "Somehow, the bear is linked to this string of crimes, but I can't seem to connect the dots."

"The bear that lives in the shadow?"

"Yes. To find the missing girl, it seems I must find the bear."

"Have you followed your vision quest?"

"I have tried, but my dreams are still…confusing."

"Try harder, Niwot. As I told you, you must learn to dream with your eyes open to find your shadow. But be forewarned, when you enter this world, you must use all the skills I have taught you."

"And there I will find the bear?"

"If your vision quest is true, you will."

"But once I track the bear into the Shadow World, how can I kill it?"

"Patience. A warrior must first define the battlefield. Your enemy will try and trick you, to draw you into a fight were he has the advantage. You must choose the time and place for battle."

"Patience," Logan repeated, "is a virtue. I've heard

that before."

"You will also need to enlist the help of your allies. Once you find them, you must have faith in them, for you hold each other's fate in your hands."

Logan thought about trusting others; that was not something he was comfortable with. He'd been alone since being banished ten years ago, and he'd survived precisely by *not* trusting others.

"You must trust your chosen allies completely. Can you do this?"

"I don't know; I've always been a loner," Logan admitted. "I'd have to completely transform myself."

"Being able to transform oneself, this is also an essential skill of stealth for a warrior. You can see that now," Ten Bears smiled.

"Like a *yee naaldlooshii*? Are you talking about skin walkers?"

"To see and not be seen, this would give you a great advantage, would it not?"

"My father used to talk about them—skin walkers, I mean."

"Your father was a great warrior with powerful medicine. He could walk without being seen, without leaving a trace. As a boy, he taught you some of his ways, did he not?"

"He tried to, but I was very young. I don't remember that much."

"His lessons are there, in your mind. If you walk with him again, they will come."

"My father was a warrior; how would he fight the bear?"

"He would say that every battle is won or lost before it begins. Once you learn the weakness of your enemy, that will become your strength."

"That one I'll have to think about."

"Think well, as it may make all the difference."

"Assuming I can see without being seen, when do I strike to kill the bear?"

"Listen to me, Niwot, this is important: When you are face to face with evil, you must call evil by its true name, and strike at the moment of your Dead Balance."

"What's that?"

"It is your point of no return. The moment when you know that only you or your enemy will survive. Trust me, you will know it when it comes."

"Dead Balance…"

"It is a moment that will come only once; there will be no second chance."

"Anything else?"

"Yes, there is one more thing. Once you enter the Shadow World to kill the bear, there is no turning back. Should you fail, you, and all with you, will be lost into shadow."

Chapter 28: Two Cups for Me

"Once you enter the Shadow World to kill the bear, there is no turning back. Should you fail, you, and all with you, will be lost into shadow."

As the ominous words of Ten Bears tumbled over in his head, Logan slumped down into his favorite leather chair at the Timberline Tea Haus.

"You must learn to dream with your eyes open to find your shadow."

Dreaming with his eyes open, tracking the bear into the Shadow World; Logan felt he could do this. But trusting others on what could likely be a one-way suicide mission? That would require some more thought—deep thought, and some tea.

As Logan typed the last few sentences on his blog, his eyes grew heavy. His thoughts swirled around Ten Bears' words as he briefly entered a dream state, only to be startled awake.

"Back again?" the waitress nudged Logan's shoulder.

"Oh…yes." Logan sat up, rubbed his eyes, and looked around at the empty teahouse. "Not too busy tonight, it seems."

"No, the off-season is always slow." The waitress leaned over to glance at Logan's computer screen. "Hmm…and what deep-seated paradox are you working on this evening?"

"Honestly?"

"I find it preferable to dishonesty."

"Well, to be honest, I think I might be going a little…insane."

Logan clicked on the computer entry that he had just posted on his *Truth Detector* blog and his words came to life, reverberating against the walls of the empty room:

"Inside every man lives a darkness, an evil part of us that gnaws away at our sanity. It shrouds our judgment in shadow as it seeks to dominate our every thought and deed. It is a voice that calls out to us at night before we go to sleep, questioning our path. It taunts us that our constant struggle is too great, too emotionally consuming, our problems too overwhelming, so much so that the only peace we can possibly find is by succumbing to its message of mistrust and relinquishing our troubled life.

How does it begin, you ask? It inevitably starts with the evil that lives inside us, planting subtle seeds of doubt. It continues relentlessly, night after night, like water dripping on a stone. Ultimately, the voice of doubt finds a crack of weakness in our mind; it seeps in, and we start to believe its twisted message that no one else can ease our suffering. No matter how loud we scream out in our silence, no one can hear us, no one can help us, no one can save us. Left unchecked, it is an evil that festers in our paranoid psyche, and eventually it consumes us. Literally."

"Insanity that supplicates suicide…that's a blow to the head right out of the gate. So, let's not pull any punches. What makes you think you're insane?"

Logan paused, tapping his teacup nervously, weighing whether to unload the accumulating baggage he'd been dragging around for years, or just to make small talk. Honesty, the waitress had requested it. What the hell, the load he was carrying in secret wasn't getting any lighter.

"OK, here's my definition of insanity. I'm trying to solve a kidnapping; I hear voices in my head, and apparently, if I can't transform myself from a loner to a team player, my fragile world will collapse. And I'm sworn to secrecy about everything I just said, so the mere fact that I disclosed what I just said may cost me my job as the sheriff's consultant, or get me exiled from this world... or both."

"Trust me, I will never tell a living soul. My lips are sealed, but it sounds like I better put on another pot of tea."

"I trust you," Logan said as he put his head in his hands. "But you'd better pour two cups for me, and leave the kettle."

The waitress listened patiently as Logan recounted the strange events of the crime spree that began with the hanging at Spirit Lake, the kidnapping at Wapiti Meadows, and the partially-eaten body that had surfaced at a particularly inappropriate moment in the local landfill. Intermittently, Logan filled in the gaps with Radio's recounts of his frequency-hopping time-shifting messages from the mysterious voice known only as Guardian.

Finally, Logan paused for a breath, took a sip of tea, and slumped back down in his chair. "Crazy, huh? I can only conclude that either I have a seriously mutated serotonin transporter gene, or I'm certifiably insane. I'm leaning toward insanity."

"Well, to be honest, that's a lot for a girl to process on one cup of tea."

"Yeah, I know," Logan exhaled, somehow relieved to have at least verbally laid down his burden, if only for a moment. "So, what do you think?"

"I'm not sure where to begin."

"That's the problem; it's like I'm pulling on a rope that's not tied to anything."

The waitress stood up, freshened Logan's tea, and then put down the kettle. "Where to begin..." She tapped the teapot. "OK, you said that you're a loner."

"I always have been. That feeling is kind of hard to change, by the way."

"Yes, but feelings can change once you explore different behaviors; we'll come back to that. You mentioned this man, Radio. He seems to be a loner as well."

"Right, he doesn't talk to anyone."

"But he talks to you."

"He does, but that just started. He sent me a message, so Raven and I went to visit him."

"And have you spoken to him since?"

"Several times. In a roundabout way, he's helping me on my case."

"You said that you're talking with him about the case, so technically, he's not alone anymore. It would appear he's helping you, and now you're helping him."

"I guess."

"You're also involved in a kidnapping case?"

"Yes, the girl that was abducted at Wapiti Meadows. That's the one that concerns me the most."

"And you're trying to track her down by some spiritual means, secret tribal rituals, at great risk to yourself?"

"I think so."

"So, you're trying to help a girl you don't know, using secret techniques you're unsure of, regardless of the danger to you?"

"When you put it that way, it makes me sound pretty stupid, doesn't it?"

"Not at all, your actions seem quite altruistic."

The waitress paused, waiting for Logan to react.

"But I'm still stumped. I'm not sure I can find the answers in time to matter." Logan sighed. "And if I can't, the girl will die."

"I see...Well, if the answers are elusive, maybe you should focus on the questions. Let's come at your problem from another direction. Why does it seem that you are driven to help others, yet you refuse to ask for help yourself?"

"What?" Logan was caught off guard.

"Maybe that's the question you need ask yourself first."

Logan laughed nervously, cocked his head, and smiled.

"Are you still hearing that voice in your head?" the waitress asked.

"How did you know that?"

"Call it a hunch."

"Yes," Logan confessed. "It's getting louder. Gives me a headache sometimes."

"What does it say?"

"Honestly?"

"Honestly," the waitress pressed.

"It says that maybe the world would be better off...without me in it."

The waitress sighed, stood, and touched Logan on the shoulder.

"Look, we all have voices in our head at some time, stoking our fears, creating dark thoughts. At some point, we have to fight back against those fears and accept the consequences, no matter what they are...but we don't have to do it alone."

"I know, but I'm used to going it on my own. Deep down, I know others could help, and I'm trying to find my way to that path. It's just not easy for me."

"Someone once said, 'We either hang together, or we'll hang separately.' Which path do you want to choose?"

"I'm still thinking about that."

"Trust in others, Logan. Once you do, you will control your destiny."

Chapter 29: Etch A Sketch

Henry Hyde leaned back in his chair as he sat alone in the Sheriff's Department holding room and counted the holes in the ceiling tiles. Finally, the sheriff entered the room with Logan and dropped a case folder on the table between them.

"It looks like your trail of tears ends here," the sheriff announced as she flipped the driver's license photos of two dead bodies onto the table in front of the funeral director. "Recognize these guys?"

Henry Hyde leaned forward, studied the pictures, and then laughed. "That little liar cost me my job," he said as he pointed to the boy's picture. He picked up the photo of the body found at Spirit Lake, nodded his head, and tossed the picture back across the table.

"Oh, and look! There's his partner in crime: the cowardly lion who believed their pack of lies."

Sheriff Martin glanced at Logan and then pushed a reconstructed facial sketch of the partially-eaten body found at the landfill in front of Henry Hyde.

"What about this guy?"

After glancing at the drawing, Henry Hyde resumed his ceiling tile inspection.

"Nice Etch A Sketch. Never seen him, must be camera shy. Why do you ask?"

The sheriff stacked the photos neatly and placed them back in the folder.

"Because they're all dead, that's why. We found one up at Spirit Lake, one in Wapiti Meadows, and the last guy? We found most of him in a dumpster."

"Serves the first two right, the lying bastards."

"You have no remorse for their deaths?"

"Remorse? None whatsoever. Good riddance to bad rubbish, I'd say." Henry Hyde leaned forward over the table, motioning the sheriff to come closer. "Those two losers concocted false charges against me; made me out to be some kind of monster. I lost my job, my life, and now I'm labeled as a registered sex offender. Try explaining that on a job application or your online dating profile."

"You're breaking my heart," Sheriff Martin smirked.

"Yeah, I know. Women run from me; guys want to kick my ass."

"And to take your revenge, I think you killed them."

"Killed them? No. Did I *want to* kill them? Sure I did. They deserve to suffer for what they did to me."

"So you admit it then?"

"I admit to nothing, Sheriff. Yes, I thought about killing them, but then realized I just had to let it go; their lies were consuming me. I needed to move on, and moving up here was my way of wiping the slate clean."

"You expect me to believe that you just forgave the bastards that you say ruined your life, got religion, and moved to the mountains for some fresh air?"

"Exactly. Turned the page, started over, moved on to obscurity. Nobody knows me here because I'm just another blue-collar redneck in a dead-end job, stuck in this high country hinterland. It's a step backwards, but I've made my peace with that."

Sheriff Martin pushed back from the table and stood over Henry Hyde.

"For the record, you're claiming you had nothing

to do with any of their deaths?"

"Not claiming it, Sheriff, stating it as fact. My new mantra is, 'Live and let die,' you know… it's kind of the creed for us backwoods funeral directors. We've even got T-shirts if you want one. What size are you? I'll even give you the 'I work with dead guys' discount."

The sheriff walked over and looked out the window at the bustling streets of tourists milling about downtown.

Logan had held his tongue as long as he could stand—time was running out.

"Eighteen hours," he whispered to the sheriff as he tapped his watch.

Billie Sue Martin nodded her head and turned back to Hyde. She leaned down and whispered in his ear. "What a complete load of bull crap. You say you've found your peace? Well, you know what I think? I think you messed with the wrong hayseed up here, my friend," she said, slamming her fist on the table. "My mountain justice will bring the hammer down hard and fast on a scumbag like you."

Henry Hyde smiled, leaning back in his chair. "You and I both know you can't hang anything on me, Sheriff. I'm innocent."

"Maybe you are, and maybe you're not," Billie Sue smiled as she walked around the room. "Here's what I do think, Doctor. I think I've got enough circumstantial evidence to charge you with killing the kid. I think I'll lock you up in County while I figure out your twisted tale of woe. And now that I think about it some more, I think when I send you down to County, you'll discover that they have an overpopulation of really mean, sadistic killers in there. And you know what else? They don't have enough guards to keep track of what's going on. When I throw a piece of white meat like you in there, labeled as a kid killer, you won't last a week. That's what I think."

"Good thinking, Sheriff," Logan injected.

"My case gets closed, and I get to do a lot less paperwork," Sheriff Martin announced, closing her folder.

Henry Hyde fidgeted nervously in his chair and then stood up. "All right, wait. I didn't kill anyone. I'll tell you what I know, but I want immunity."

"Spill it and then we'll talk," the sheriff said, opening her notepad.

"I know about...the last guy, the one in the dumpster. I worked on him."

"Worked on him?"

"Yeah, I embalmed him. Well, parts of him."

"Go on." The sheriff sat down with her pad and clicked her pen.

"It's like this; I get bodies sent up here from County sometimes. Overflow, they call it."

"Overflow?"

"The morgue at County gets backed up and can't handle their load—budget cutbacks, you know. So they ship me a body or two every now and then, off the books. I take care of it; they bill it out, collect from the state, and throw me a kickback. They look efficient, and I make a few bucks on the side."

"And the dead guys tell no tales?"

"Exactly. Where's the harm?"

"These bodies you get, what do you do with them?"

"That's the crazy thing. Someone on the Internet's always looking for a dead body."

"So you sell the dead bodies on the black market?"

"Sell dead bodies? That sounds kind of creepy. I consider it more like...recycling. It's the new normal, Sheriff."

The sheriff put down her pen, stood up, and looked out the window again at the happy faces of holiday shoppers shuffling down the street. *Oblivion, it looked like a nice place to visit.*

"OK, so how did your dead guy get in my dumpster?"

"Beats me, you should ask the ranger."

"The ranger? Why her?"

"Because after I embalmed him, she picked up the body."

"What? Why would she do that?"

"Don't know, don't care. In my...extracurricular line of work, you don't ask questions."

"Then give me the details. What actually happened?"

"OK, the ranger shows up one night, says she was there to pick up a body. Said it was all arranged and paid for. Sure enough, there was an unmarked envelope with two grand in my mail slot—cash."

"And you didn't think that was strange?"

"Sure it was, but a man's got to pay his bills, and I don't get enough regular bodies up here to do that. You know what they say: Don't look a gift horse in the mouth."

"Just a little free black market enterprise at work?"

"Exactly. That's my story, so I get immunity, right? You said I'd get immunity."

"If your story checks out, maybe. Just one more thing, Mr. Hyde...What does a park ranger need with a dead body?"

"How would I know?" Henry Hyde replied,

leaning back in his chair. "Maybe you should ask her."

"I think I will."

Chapter 30: How Can I Help You?

"Get me park service headquarters," Sheriff Martin barked as she marched down the hall. "Now!"

The startled dispatcher put down her buffalo burger, brushed the crumbs from her uniform, and punched in the number. "On speaker now, sir."

"Park service, how can I help you?"

"This is Sheriff Martin down in Deadraven," Billie Sue began. "Let me speak with Ranger Supervisor Burns."

"I'm sorry, Sheriff, he's not in. Would you like to leave a message?"

"Who am I speaking with?"

"This is Tammy Morgan, visitor services intern. Everyone else left early because of the storm."

"OK, Ms. Morgan, you'll do. I need to locate one of your rangers. Ranger Summerhill—it's important."

The intern sat back down at her desk and turned on her vintage computer.

"Yes, Sheriff. Let me check the logs. OK, Ranger Summerhill…here we are. She called in a poacher sighting yesterday on one of the upper peaks, Sawtooth Ridge, I believe. I hate poachers, don't you?"

"We all hate them, Ms. Morgan. Where's the ranger right now?"

"She's out on backcountry patrol."

"Can you reach her?"

"I don't know, Sheriff. She hasn't reported in today."

Billie Sue Martin took a deep breath, and then redirected her questioning. "OK, where do you *think* she is?"

"Well, I'm new here, Sheriff, but there's five hundred thousand acres of wilderness up here along the divide. Your guess is as good as mine."

"Can you call her?"

"There's no cell coverage up here. Most of the rangers turn their phones off to save the battery."

Sheriff Martin glanced at the dispatcher with her mouth full of buffalo and frowned. "Does she carry a walkie?"

"Yes, she does! But reception up on the divide is pretty spotty even in good weather. I doubt I could reach her in this storm."

Logan had listened patiently but had to interrupt. "Aren't all rangers required to carry a tracker beacon?"

"Let me see…Here we are, new policy. Yes, they are. She checked one out and activated it… yesterday."

"So you can at least track her. Now we're getting somewhere."

"Hmm, that's strange," the intern mumbled as she clicked to the tracker map on her computer.

"Where's her tracker location?" Billie Sue insisted.

"This has to be wrong, Sheriff."

"What do you mean?"

"The tracker data doesn't make any sense. Her beacon was activated yesterday, and then it appears she deactivated it."

Billie Sue looked up at the ceiling. "OK, when did she turn it on?"

"At our office. Actually, I turned it on for her when I handed it to her."

"And when did she turn it off?"

There was a brief silence.
"Ten minutes later."

Chapter 31: Who is Who?

"You're right," Sheriff Martin reflected. "That doesn't make any sense. Why would a ranger, headed into the backcountry, turn her tracker off within ten minutes of activation?"

"No, it doesn't," the intern agreed. "Make sense, I mean."

"Can you identify where it was turned off?"

The intern studied the computer screen, zooming in on the map. "Oh, that's a new function! I just learned how to do that, the tracker was deactivated at...her ranger cabin, just down the road."

"Maybe she saw the storm coming in and decided to wait it out," Sheriff Martin offered. "Can you raise her on her walkie?"

"Trying now," the intern said, as she stood up from her desk and cleared a small circle of condensation on the window. "No answer. But she must be there; I can see a light on."

"Can you walk down to the cabin? I need to speak to her."

Standing alone in the office, the intern looked out the window of park headquarters; the snow was coming down harder and the light in the ranger's cabin flickered in the wind.

"The storm's getting worse, Sheriff," the intern responded in a worried voice. "I need to leave soon or I could get stuck up here. She probably decided to stay and just left the light on."

"Yeah," Billie Sue agreed, "she's curled up with a good book having a cup of tea. But just for the record,

I need you to go check on her."

There was an uneasy silence on the other end of the line.

"It will only take a few minutes," Sheriff Martin coaxed.

"All right," the intern sighed. "Let me shut down here so I can be ready to leave. I'll get my boots on and check the cabin on my way out."

"I appreciate it, Ms. Morgan. I'll hold," Sheriff Martin said, as she signaled the dispatcher to mute the call.

Chapter 32: Isolation

"What's up with the cloak-and-dagger routine?" Logan asked.

"Beats me," Billie Sue exclaimed. "Something's not right here."

Before Logan could respond, a blinking red light on the switchboard interrupted their discussion.

"I'll see if she's in," the dispatcher responded, muting the call. "It's Sheriff Daniel Johnson from Blackrock County. Are you in?"

"Put him through," Billie Sue acknowledged.

"Hey, Sheriff, how's it going up there?" Sheriff Johnson blurted out.

"It's minus five degrees and snowing like a son of a bitch," Billie Sue rattled off. "Chamber of Commerce Day. Great time for a little weekend getaway for you and the kids, don't you think?"

"Well, I'm watching this storm on the Weather Channel, so I may have to pass on that holiday for now. Listen, Sheriff, there are two reasons I'm calling. First off, we're closing the road up the mountain to Deadraven and the National Park. Don't want to risk getting any tourists stranded up there."

"That's our only lifeline, Danny boy. We'll be cut off."

"I am sorry about that, Sheriff, but it's just too dangerous."

"All right, how long?"

"Oh, only a couple of days, most likely. Weather should break in forty-eight hours or so. I know you got your little Winter Festival and all, but I'm afraid the tourists will just have to stay down here for all their holiday shopping this year. It's unfortunate for you, but we can use the business—it's been a tough year."

"Appreciate your concern, Sheriff. Especially for the safety of the tourists, and their wallets."

"Just doing my job."

"You said two things…"

"Oh, yeah. I wanted to give you a heads-up. Just got a report on an escaped mental patient from County. Assaulted her therapist three weeks ago and fled."

"Three weeks ago? That one's a little stale, don't you think? Things moving slow down there?"

"Yeah, getting to be more like you guys, I'm afraid. Must be on mountain time."

"Thanks for the belated heads-up."

"Listen, Sheriff, I'm over here at the hospital right now with the victim, taking my report. He just regained consciousness; that's why I'm calling you directly on this one."

"What happened?"

"I'm still trying to piece this one together. Seems our perp whacked her therapist on the head, grabbed his keys, and just walked out the front door. She found his SUV in the parking lot and drove away; left the poor doc here in a coma for three weeks."

"I'd like to help you with your slow-motion crime wave, Danny, but that sounds like your problem. I've got a missing girl I'm looking for up here—kind of urgent."

"Yeah, I heard about your murder-slash-kidnapping, Sheriff. That's why I'm calling. I think my fugitive may have headed up your way."

"Why would you think that?"

"My new forensics team was examining the log

books at the hospital. You don't have a forensics team up there, do you, Sheriff?"

"No, we don't. But I have a CSi."

"How did you get a CSI on your budget?"

"Well, actually he's a crime scene *intern*, a volunteer, little *i*. But he's one dead body bird dog, I'm telling you."

"OK, whatever. Anyway, my new forensics team noticed that the perpetrator only had one regular visitor for the last ten years. Same day, every month, every year, regular as clockwork."

"And who would that be?" Billie Sue asked.

"Someone from your little mountain paradise, actually. Seems my fugitive down here has a sister up there: Karen Summerhill, she's a ranger up in the park…your park, that is."

"I'm sending you a picture of my fugitive now. The boys down here call her the Prom Queen; they always slap the funniest handles on our more notorious felons. Thought you might want to keep an eye out for her."

Logan and Billie Sue Martin moved closer to computer as the picture from Sheriff Johnson appeared on the dispatcher's screen. They exchanged a confused glance and stepped back.

"I know this woman," Billie Sue acknowledged. "But that doesn't make any sense. She's a ranger up here in the park we've been working with—Ranger Summerhill."

There was a strange pause on the other end of the call. "You sure about that, Sheriff?"

"I'd bet my life on it," Billie Sue exclaimed. "I'm working three crimes with her right now."

"Really?" Sheriff Johnson questioned. "The picture

is of *Sharon* Summerhill; she's been locked up down here in a mental institution for the last ten years."

"Your escaped mental patient, what was she locked up for?"

"The Prom Queen? Oh, that's right, you wouldn't remember her; I forget you're not a local sometimes. Was on all on the networks back in the day. High school tragedy, it was, the newspeople called her the Prom Queen Killer."

"Killer? What did she do?"

"It seems she and her sister, the one that's been visiting her? They were real close, you know. So close that when our mental patient's sister ran for prom queen her senior year, she'd been queen for three years running. Well, she came up against some serious competition that last year. When it looked like she was going to lose her crown, our future mental patient wigged out, kidnapped the girl running against her sister for queen, and killed her."

"Why would she do that?"

"Why do kids do anything these days? Low self-esteem, drugs, Mommy didn't love her…Hell, I don't know. I just get the call when they go off the reservation."

"How did she kill the kidnapped girl?" Logan interrupted.

"Now, that's the thing. They found her body in an old, abandoned mineshaft outside of town, with my escaped mental patient pacing around the body, talking to the dead girl. Looked like she kept her alive for twenty-four hours and then shot her point-blank, right between the eyes, the day after the prom. Funny thing, in all these years, she remained silent about the whole thing. Never admitted to the killing, much less told anyone why."

"That is creepy," Sheriff Martin observed.

"Silent, she was, until three weeks ago. Seems our prom queen heard some kind of voice in her head and spilled it all to her therapist. Confessed to the kidnapping and killing."

"And you think she's headed this way?" Billie Sue repeated.

Logan made a cutting gesture with his hand across his throat.

"Can you hold the line, Sheriff?"

"Sure thing."

Chapter 33: Double Take

"I'm getting a bad feeling here," Logan exhaled.

"Me too," Sheriff Martin echoed as she turned to the dispatcher. "Get Ms. Morgan back on the line."

The dispatcher punched a blinking light on her screen, nodded, and patched the park intern back on speaker.

"Good, I caught you," the sheriff began cautiously. "Is your computer still up?"

"Yes, Sheriff. I was just about to shut it down. I have to get going, really."

"This won't take long. I need you to take a look at something for me."

Billie Sue motioned for the dispatcher to forward the photograph to the park intern Sheriff Johnson had sent of the escaped mental patient.

"Tammy, have you ever seen this woman?"

The intern clicked on the photo; she was confused. "Of course, Sheriff, that's Ranger Summerhill."

"Are you sure?"

"Yes, I met her yesterday when she checked out her tracker. I already told you, I helped her activate it. She said she hadn't used one of these new models, so I showed her how it worked."

"What else did she say to you? When she picked up the tracker, I mean."

"She said she was headed up the mountain to look for poachers."

"Anything else?"

"Yes, she forgot the key to her gear locker, so I opened it for her."

"And?"

"She retrieved her service weapon, a forty-five caliber pistol. Said she didn't want to go tracking poachers with just a radio."

The intern looked out the window; the snow was coming down heavily now. "Sheriff, we've been over this before, and the storm is getting worse. I need to…"

"And you'd never seen her before yesterday? Ranger Summerhill, I mean."

There was brief silence on the line followed by a bit of static. "To be honest, Sheriff, she's the only ranger I've met. They each have their own cabins, but they only check in here at the office about once a month. I started working here three weeks ago. My dad's a friend of the park supervisor and he got me this last-minute internship for winter break. Based on my grades, I need this credit to graduate next summer."

"What about Supervisor Burns?"

"My boss? I haven't met him either, but he's called me on the phone a few times. He's a nice man."

Sheriff Martin looked at Logan.

"OK, Ms. Morgan, can you check the personnel database?"

"I think so. I'm a computer major, you know."

"That's great. Look up the ranger profiles for me."

"Doing it now."

"Does the picture I sent you match any of the rangers in your file?"

"Hum…that's strange. She's not there. How can that be? She had a badge, Sheriff…and a name tag. It takes a month to get those name tags made; I just ordered some new ones."

"OK, listen to me, Tammy," Sheriff Martin proceeded cautiously. "Is the light still on at the ranger's cabin?"

The park intern stood up from her desk and parted the blinds on the window. It was snowing hard, but she could still make out the flickering porch light.

"Uh, yes it is."

"Good. I know there's a storm, but I need you to go the ranger's cabin now and see if she is there. Can you do that?"

"Her light's on; why wouldn't she be there? You're starting to scare me, Sheriff."

"I don't want to frighten you, Tammy, but I just learned the roads down the mountain are closed, so you're going to be there for a little bit. I'm sending one of my deputies in a Snowcat to pick you up, but he can't get there for a few hours in this storm."

"You mean…I'm trapped up here?"

"You're not trapped, just stuck for a while. We'll get you home. My dispatcher will stay on the phone with you until the deputy arrives."

Sheriff Martin motioned for the dispatcher to mute the call.

"You sure this is a good idea?" Logan whispered.

"We've got no other choice," Billie Sue responded.

The dispatcher waved her hand to signal she was putting the intern back on speaker.

"I want to leave now, Sheriff," the intern sobbed.

"Tammy, listen to me," Billie Sue stated calmly. "You've heard about that missing girl from Wapiti Meadows?"

"The one who was…kidnapped?"

"Yes, her. We're trying to find her right now. We think your ranger may know something about her disappearance, and we need to talk to her."

The phone went silent, and then the intern spoke

softly. "I just want to go home, Sheriff."

"Tammy, the girl who was kidnapped is about your age. We think she's still alive, but if she's out there in this storm, she won't be for... You can help us find her, Tammy. You want to help that missing girl, don't you?"

"Yes...How can I help?" the intern sniffed.

"I told you, Tammy, we need to ask Ranger Summerhill some questions."

"She's probably not down there; she just left the lights on, Sheriff. She said she was going to the backcountry looking for poachers."

"Maybe she's not there, but we need you to find out for sure. If she's on the mountain, maybe she left a map, a note...something that will help us find her. And we need her help to find the missing girl."

There was a long silence on the line.

"Are you still with me, Tammy?"

"Yes."

"Go down to the cabin, Tammy," Billie Sue repeated, "and tell me what you find."

"Your deputy's on the way, right?"

"Yes, he's on the way. And I'm here with you."

The intern wiped her eyes, opened the door into the blowing snow and stumbled down the snow-covered road toward the dim porch light of the ranger's cabin. The wind howled through the trees, causing her to grasp the porch railing to keep from being blown over into a snowbank.

"OK, I'm at the cabin!"

"Can you see anybody inside?" the sheriff asked.

The intern rubbed the ice from the window and peered into the dark cabin. "No, I can't see anything. She's not here; I'm going back."

"I need you to check inside, Tammy."

The intern turned the door handle and nervously shoved her foot across the threshold. A gust of wind blew snow through the kitchen as it ruffled the curtains. Several windows were open in the back of the cabin, and it was freezing inside.

"Is anyone here?"

There was no answer.

Walking cautiously through the entryway, the young girl noticed a dim light coming from the bedroom. She crept across the entryway and slowly pushed the bedroom door open. As the shimmering porch light danced through the window shades, it caught the silhouette of a frozen body on the floor, its empty, lifeless eyes staring at the ceiling. Tammy gasped, unable to breathe as she stumbled back onto the front porch, trying to catch her breath. "There's a...d-dead woman in there!"

"Who's dead?"

"It's Ranger Summerhill! Not the Ranger Summerhill I met, the Ranger Summerhill from the database file."

"Tammy? Listen to me carefully. Go back to the park office and lock the door. Do you know how to use a gun?"

"Yes." The intern tried to breathe. "I grew up on a ranch, I can shoot. But I mostly shot tin cans on the fence with my dad's rifle, that's all. I could hit some of them."

"That's good, Tammy. Go back to the office. There's a gun cabinet in the hallway. Supervisor Burns always keeps the key on top of the cabinet. Unlock the cabinet; get a shotgun and some shells out. Can you do that?"

"Yes, Sheriff," Tammy sobbed as she ran back up

the road.

"You lock yourself in the bathroom until my deputy comes. His name is Brad. Don't open the door for anyone except for Brad, and he'll come and get you. Do you understand me, Tammy?"

"Yes, Brad. No one but Brad," Tammy panted as she reached the office and threw open the door. She grabbed a shotgun and a box of shells from the gun cabinet, ducked into the bathroom, and slammed the door. Collapsing to the floor, Tammy tore open the box of shells and shoved three rounds into the magazine.

"Are you OK, Tammy?"

"I'm OK now," the intern answered, catching her breath as she cocked the shotgun.

"Good. Deputy Brad will be there soon."

"Sheriff?" Tammy asked as she double-checked the lock on the door.

"Yes, Tammy?"

"I will get extra credit for this, won't I?"

"I'm sure you will."

Chapter 34: New News

Sheriff Martin leaned over the dispatcher and hit the mute button for the phone. She paced over to the window for a moment, processing the news of a dead park ranger and the shotgun-toting intern now barricaded inside the bathroom, awaiting rescue by Deputy Brad. Like sands through an hourglass, the odds of finding the kidnapped girl before she was frozen to death or murdered rapidly were slipping away. She spun around and punched another button on the dispatch console.

"Sheriff Johnson, you still on the line?"

"I'm here, Sheriff. You had me on hold long enough to get the report back on that nine millimeter you sent down to my new forensics team."

Billie Sue didn't respond; she was in no mood for a dick-measuring contest today.

"OK, Sheriff, your gun was registered to one Dr. Malcolm Kennedy, a hospital administrator over in Fort Morgan. Odd, I believe I saw your accident report on him a few weeks back, seems he took a tumble in the park."

"Uh, yes, that was my report. Interesting, Sheriff, he didn't have a gun on him when we found his body."

"Well, yes, that was interesting. But here is where it gets, shall we say, more interesting, Sheriff. Dr. Kennedy's gun, the gun you sent me? We matched it to the bullet you sent us; it's the gun that killed your kid at Wapiti Meadows."

"I knew it! We found that gun in a suspect's backpack a week ago, but I had to cut him loose. I'll bring him in."

"I wouldn't do that just yet, Sheriff."

"Why not?"

"The gun and shell casings had been wiped clean—no fingerprints."

"Yeah, we already knew that."

"But we did find some trace DNA evidence from the shooter on the trigger. It's not a match with your outlaw."

"What? Are you sure?"

"We're running more tests now, but I can tell you one thing for sure: The DNA on the murder weapon, it's not from your guy."

"Why would you say that?"

"Because the DNA is female."

"What? That can't be…"

"DNA doesn't lie, Sheriff. Also, I'm looking at the ballistics report in front of me, the one from my forensics team. The killer you're looking for, *she* used this gun."

Billie Sue Martin took a breath and scratched her head; none of this made sense.

"And just for future reference, whenever you punch those fancy buttons on your dispatch panel, we can still hear you down here—all of you. We've been listening in on the rest of your park service drama, and my assault victim has something to contribute. Says it might be important."

Sheriff Martin shot an angry glance at the dispatcher, and she shrugged. "OK, put him on."

"Sheriff, my patient drifted in and out of catatonia for years until we recently began shock therapy for her schizophrenia. It was working; she began to recover memories from her past, and that's when she confessed to the kidnap and killing of another girl, ten years ago. She told me that she heard a voice in her head, and the voice told her to do it—kill the girl, I mean."

"I'm listening."

"She said that the only person she ever confessed the killing to, other than me, was her sister, the park ranger. My patient also told me that her sister implored her to keep everything about the killings secret, to herself, and she did, Sheriff, for ten years. Her sister, the park ranger, came to visit her every month. The ranger shared her life with her, everything about working for the park service. They were very close, those two. Other than her sister, my patient had no other contact with the outside world."

"Why didn't Ranger Summerhill tell anyone up here about her past? She had a sibling that committed a crime and she was trying to stay connected to her. There's no shame in that," Billie Sue offered.

"I don't know, Sheriff. That part is confusing to me as well. Mental illness carries a negative stigma in our society, but it is a treatable illness."

"Look, Doc, you had your patient in therapy for ten years. Was she ever a threat during all that time?"

"No, she was not, but then something happened around three weeks ago that changed everything."

"What happened?"

"She said she had a terrible nightmare…and the voice came back."

"The voice?"

"The voice that told her to do bad things. The voice that told her to kidnap that girl ten years ago and kill her."

"So, she's starting to remember what she's done?" Sheriff Martin exhaled. "That's good, isn't it? Don't you have to own your sins to begin some kind of cathartic thing in psychotherapy? You know, find your first step to recovery?"

"Normally, as you say, it is a good thing, Sheriff, but that's not why I'm sharing this information with you."

"OK, Doc, why are you telling me this?"

"Because the voice in her head, the one that told her to kidnap that girl ten years ago and kill her?"

"Yes?"

"It told her to do it again."

Chapter 35: Outbound

"Damn it!" Sheriff Martin slammed her fist down on the table, startling the dispatcher.

"This thing is going downhill fast," Logan added.

"We've got to find that ranger imposter! Now!"

"What about Search and Rescue?" the dispatcher asked.

"Not an option," Logan responded, as he clicked through the incoming storm pattern on the Weather Channel. "They can't provide air support in these winds. Whiteout conditions along the divide, terrain's too rough for snow machines or horses, and we'd never get a team on foot up there in time."

"Her sister was a ranger," Sheriff Martin said as she paced the room, "and they shared everything, including their dark past. We'll come back to that one later."

"A voice sets her off," Logan continued the line of thought. "She kills her sister, kidnaps a girl, and now she thinks she's the ranger."

"I don't care who she thinks she is," the sheriff pondered. "Right now, all I care about is finding the girl before she finishes whatever that voice inside her head started. So, where the hell is she going?"

"There are a few backcountry shelters along the divide."

"Go on," Sheriff Martin scrambled to pull out a park service map from the desk.

"Six of them, spread out across the peaks."

"Show me."

"They're not on that map," Logan hesitated. "Or

any map. The park service never publishes where they are. Partially because they're next to the Shadow Mountain Reservation; spiritual lands, off-limits for outsiders. But I think the main reason is that they just don't want any tourists tromping around up there, trespassing on tribal lands. Bad medicine, Sheriff, and outside your jurisdiction."

Billie Sue pushed the map aside. "Jurisdiction I understand, but bad medicine? What the hell do I do with that?"

"Look, Sheriff, I know where the shelters are; I've hiked them all."

"OK, if you were our escaped mental patient, where would you go?"

Logan rubbed his chin, studying the map of the backcountry.

"She'll have to take shelter until the storm blows through. Too much snow to build one."

"Six places to look," Billie Sue barked. "We couldn't find one in this weather."

Logan glanced at his watch.

Five PM, sixteen hours since Wapiti Meadows.

"Our kidnap victim is either alone, freezing to death on the mountain, or holed up with a lunatic killer. If we don't find her soon," the sheriff sighed, "she's dead."

Logan looked out the window; the howling wind was pushing the snow sideways.

"No one's going anywhere, Sheriff, until this storm breaks."

"So wherever those two are now, you think they'll be there tomorrow?"

"I don't know about our missing girl," Logan sighed, looking out the window at the raging storm.

"But based on our ranger imposter's history with kidnap victims, tomorrow may never come."

Chapter 36: What Are You?

High along the Continental Divide, a noisy crackle of static broke through the howling winds as the lights on Radio's scanner pulsated in the darkness. Instinctively, he switched on his recorder and creaked across the room, rotating the frequency knob to get a better signal as he scribbled down the message.

5:07 PM, 25 degrees below zero.

Between the static, the barely audible signal faded in and out.

"Hi, Mom and Dad, we're both fine! Thanks for the tracker, Dad! We love the mountains!"

The voice that haunted Radio's airwaves and dreams repeated its message twice, and then faded into the ether as mysteriously as it appeared. He sat there for a moment, rubbed his eyes and exhaled. Something was different this time. Glancing at the log, he replayed the transmission and listened intently to the squeal of the frequency-hopping scanner, trying to pinpoint the anomaly.

"What are you up to, Guardian?" he mumbled. Rotating the dials on the scanner, he locked in on the frequency, comparing it to the recording. "There!" he blurted out. "But that doesn't make any sense," he said, rechecking his log. "You're not an Internet transmission…you're a… *satellite?* Not a GPS satellite, something else altogether. What are you?"

Launching his chair across the room, Radio banged away at his computers, trying to identify the source of the satellite signal. From the ground-based telemetry, he projected the location of the geosynchronous satellite-positioning packet embedded in the message. "Hello, GEOS," Radio smiled. "What the hell is the IERCC trying to tell me?"

Just as he was triangulating the satellite signal to its ground-based source, the signal, just like Guardian's message, surged, and then was gone. "Damn it! Come back!"

Radio whirled around in his chair, lost for a moment in his frustration. "Truth Detector," he blurted into his microphone. "She's back…"

The vibration of Logan's phone in his pocket pulled him away from the window in the sheriff's station. "I'm listening," Logan responded.

"She's back…but she's different this time; it makes no sense. Listen."

Logan strained to hear the faint voice he now knew as Guardian as it replayed from Radio's recording. *"Hi, Mom and Dad, we're both fine! Thanks for the tracker, Dad! We love the mountains!"*

Radio was right, Logan thought. *It didn't make any sense.* He turned to the sheriff and scratched his head before responding.

"OK, my friend, let's think. You keep track of who's in your neighborhood, don't you?"

"You know I do."

"Who else could be out there? Any free climbers on the mountain today?"

"In this weather? They'd be frozen meat in this storm."

"You said the message was…different. But it was from Guardian, right?"

"It *is* Guardian, yes, I'm sure of it. But this time, the message, it's different."

"What's different?"

"This one's got an embedded GEOS data channel and a time stamp. And it's not right!"

"What do you mean?"

"She usually gives me an advance notice when something bad is going down, you know, time to react. I always guessed she was giving me a glimpse into the future, like some kind of a test, to see if I would *do* something...if I only knew what to do."

"And now?"

"Now the time stamp is in the *past*."

"What?"

"What am I supposed to do with that? I can't change the past!"

"You told me," Logan paused as he spoke softly on the phone, "you did that, you did something, maybe that's all she wanted. Keep your ears on, my friend."

"I need your computer!" Logan commanded to the dispatcher.

"OK," she responded, quickly rolling her chair out of his way.

Playing back the Guardian message, Logan isolated the embedded GEOS and completed the triangulation of the satellite signal from Radio and its ground-based source. "Good work, my friend," Logan mumbled. "You left me some bread crumbs."

With the signal connection, Logan narrowed in on the ground source device ID. "There you are! The signal came from...a portable hiking beacon."

"Can you track the owner?" Sheriff Martin asked as she leaned over the computer screen.

"Yes, here's the account, a family package registered to one Matthew Higgins. It's encrypted... but not very well. Kids' birthdays, pet names...When will people ever learn?"

"The owner's?"

"No, the daughter's. Here it is...The beacon is registered to...our missing girl's father!" Logan exclaimed as he spun around to the dispatcher. "Here's his home number."

"Get him on the line, now!" Sheriff Martin barked.

Before the dispatcher could initiate contact, her emergency screen lit up with an inbound call. The caller ID showed it was coming from the missing girl's father.

"Nine-one-one. What is your emergency?" the dispatcher answered instinctively, pointing at the inbound caller ID.

"On speaker!" Sheriff Martin shouted.

"We just got a message from Caroline," the missing girl's father gasped.

"What message?"

"It's a prerecorded message from my tracker beacon. We always set it up before she goes camping, so she can let us know she's OK. It says...Well, here it is: *Hi, Mom and Dad, we're both fine! Thanks for the tracker, Dad! We love the mountains!*"

"I don't understand," the father choked. "Why would she send that message now, saying that they're both OK? We know the boy is dead and our Caroline is missing."

"Mr. Higgins," Sheriff Martin hesitated, "hold the line." She whipped around to Logan. "Can you locate the source of that message?"

"Already on it...It's encoded in the metadata."

Pecking away at the keyboard, Logan ran his hand down the screen of data. "Here it is."

Logan pulled up the user account for the tracking device and displayed a location map of its active transmissions. "OK, she originally pinged in from…Wapiti Meadows," he pointed to the screen. "That's where she sent the prerecorded message."

"When?"

"From the time stamp, it looks like just before the attack when the boy was killed."

"And her father just got it now? How can that be?"

"I don't know. It must have bounced around in the ether for a while."

"It can do that?"

"Strangely enough, Sheriff, it can. It's kind of complicated, but the storm must be trapping the radio waves, keeping the signal alive somehow."

"What happened then?"

"The tracker engaged," Logan continued, analyzing the data. "It logged tracks for a short distance…Then the satellite lost the ground signal."

"That's it? The trail's gone?"

"That's it," Logan sighed. As Logan stared at the blinking computer screen, he couldn't help but think that if this was the end of the trail—the girl was gone. *Think!*

"The ground source device ID," Logan blurted out. "Radio, you got your ears on?"

"You know I do, Truth Detector," Radio snapped to attention.

"OK, here's what we need. You tracked the GEOS transmission, right?"

"Yes, but I lost the signal before I could triangulate the ground source."

"Not to worry, I found it. It originated from a portable tracking device. Here's the device ID."

"Got it," Radio acknowledged.

"I can't locate any more satellite communications to the device; with the storm, it probably can't get through anyway. But if the device was attempting an uplink loop, maybe some of its transmission packets are still bouncing around underneath the storm, like the ones you intercepted."

"I see where you're going," Radio smiled. "By the way, if I ever go to war again, I want you on my side. I'm on it."

There was a crackle of static as the lights dimmed in the sheriff's station. The door swung open unexpectedly, and in walked Raven.

"I've been looking all over for you," Raven announced as she squeezed herself between Logan and the sheriff, scanning the screen. "Radio contacted me and said you might need another tracker."

"It couldn't hurt," Logan smiled. "Sit down. You're pretty good at finding a trail."

"Lot of noise out there," Radio interrupted. "Cleaning up the signal. OK, she's weak, but here she is…"

Logan downloaded the transmission data, fed it into the geo-mapping device website, and suddenly, faint footprints appeared on his tracking screen.

"That's Spirit Lake trailhead!" the sheriff pointed at the screen.

"Yes, they started out northwest, past the trail boundaries and then…"

The tracks stopped.

"And then they just disappear?" Sheriff Martin observed. "What's beyond Spirit Lake in that direction?"

Logan scanned the map.

"Nothing, really. Impassable rock face along the divide one way, a glacier in the other direction…"

"What about one of those backcountry shelters?"

Raven asked.

"None. There's no shelter of any kind up there for miles."

Logan paused and exchanged a glance with Raven. "I think I know where they're headed."

"How?"

"I'll tell you on the way."

Logan grabbed the dispatch phone and punched in the number for High Country Cycles.

"Cody? Call your flyboy. I need a favor: these coordinates."

"No, 'Hello, how are you?'" Cody Winston whipped back. "You stink up my couch, I don't see you and Raven for days, and then it's, *snap*! Gimme!"

"You're right," Logan apologized. "Too fast. How's your day going?"

"Well, I didn't sleep so well last night. I'm worried about my…Oh, forget the crap, what do you need?"

"A war bird. Apache, to be specific."

"This sounds like fun. OK, when?"

"Fifteen minutes would be good. Now would be better."

"You're going to owe me for this one."

"Put it on my tab," Logan laughed.

"All right then; one war bird to go."

"What the heck was that?" Sheriff Martin puzzled.

"Just calling us a taxi," Logan snapped as he grabbed his jacket.

"A taxi?"

"Grab some ropes," Logan barked to Raven. "And an axe."

Raven smiled as she quickly commandeered two packs from the supply cabinet.

Above the sheriff's building, the deafening low

thump of helicopter blades created a sonic snow duster in the parking lot.

"Come on!" Logan yelled as he entered the stairway to the roof. "Our taxi's here."

"I thought you said Search and Rescue couldn't fly in this weather?" Sheriff Martin shouted above the dull, heavy sound of the helicopter blades.

"They can't, but we can," Logan barked back as they reached the roof. "Load up!"

As Raven and the sheriff piled into the back of the military Apache, Logan tossed his pack onboard and rotated a hand signal for the pilot to take off.

When the helicopter cleared the power lines over the sheriff's building, Cody Winston flashed a thumbs up to her flyboy pilot. Wheeling around from her copilot seat, she punched Logan on the shoulder.

"Mind telling me what's going on?" Cody roared over the drone of the chopper blades.

"Sure," Logan called back as he handed his phone to Cody, pointing at the screen. "We need to go here. Now!" As Cody Winston shared the GPS coordinates with the pilot, he shook his head and mouthed something back to Cody.

"Really?" Cody screeched as she looked back to Logan. "I hope you know what you're doing, man."

The helicopter dipped abruptly and changed course directly into the oncoming storm, heading through the canyons deep into the Rocky Mountains.

"OK, bird dog," the sheriff inquired impatiently. "Spill."

Logan motioned for the sheriff and Raven to huddle together so he could be heard over the whirr of the helicopter blades.

"I know where the ranger is taking the kidnapped

girl," Logan said.

"How?"

"The girl's tracker beacon left a trail from Spirit Lake into the mountains, right?"

"Right," Sheriff Martin shouted.

"Well, there's nowhere up there to get out of the storm."

Raven exchanged a glance with Logan and smiled. "Except the old cave on Thunderbird Mountain!"

"Exactly," Logan answered.

"You two want to tell me what's going on?" Sheriff Martin asked.

"OK," Logan explained. "The ranger's dead, killed by her sister. The therapist told us that his patient escaped after she heard a voice that told her to, 'Do it again.'"

"I follow you so far…"

"The ranger imposter kidnapped the girl, and now she's taking her to a secure location—a location that only a real ranger would know about, one away from any of the known shelters, one that's not on any map."

"But how do you know she's headed for this old cave?"

"'Just like before,'" Logan repeated the therapist's words. "That's what the voice told her. She killed the last girl in an old, abandoned mineshaft outside of town. A mineshaft—a cave, a secluded place, away from everyone…just like before. Her ranger sister must have told her about the unmarked cave up on the mountain. That's where she's taking the girl."

The helicopter lurched sideways as the pilot traversed between two rocky peaks in an air pocket. Logan crawled forward and pointed out the side window at a small flat spot on an icy glacier ahead.

"We need to get out over there!" he shouted above the noise of the engine.

"Too rough in these crosswinds!" the pilot shouted back. "Can't land there!"

"I can do it," Cody Winston interrupted as she grabbed the pilot's hand on the controls. "Give it to me!"

"What makes you think I'd do that?" the pilot snapped as he wrestled control away from his copilot.

"Because I can fly this beast, and you know it!"

"Really?"

"How many sorties have I flown with you in *Passage to Niburu*? Hundreds of missions over enemy territory; never ditched once!"

The pilot turned to Cody, lifting his visor. "Affirmative, you're a great pilot, but that's a sci-fi video game, on the sofa in your shop. This is for real."

"It's the same video game you use to train your weekend warriors, knucklehead! The same video game where I can outfly anyone in your frickin' squadron."

"It's not happening!"

"You want your bike back, right?" Cody moved close to the flyboy.

The pilot hovered above the rock face, listening for what he knew was about to become an offer he couldn't refuse. "Go on."

"Me, and the Knucklehead. I fly the chopper, and you get a ride."

"A ride?"

"Yeah, both of us, up in the park. *Comprende?*"

The pilot released his hand from the controls and grinned.

"OK, Flygirl, you know how to yank my joystick. But you crash my bird, and I'll kill you."

"If you two are about done with the foreplay," Logan interrupted, pointing to the glacier below, "we need to get off, too...right over there. Now!"

"Sure thing," Cody said as she swooped the chopper down to a small patch of ice between the jagged rocks of the glacier.

As Raven tossed the climbing gear out of the helicopter, Logan leaned forward and whispered in Cody's ear, "I owe you one, girl."

"I know, I know. Put it on your tab," Cody shot back. "But it's more than one this time."

"I hate to hit and run," the pilot interrupted, "but I've got to get this bird back to base before it's missed."

"You don't have clearance for this flight plan, knucklehead?" Cody shouted.

"Technically, no."

"Then let go of the stick," Cody smiled. "I'll drive. We'll get there faster."

As the Apache war bird lurched away upwards between the rock face and the mountain, Sheriff Martin stood on a precipice, looked down at the icy rocks below and turned to Logan.

"I'm guessing your hidden cave is over that cliff of doom there?"

"That's why we brought the riggings," Logan shouted as he looped a support rope on a boulder and clamped the three together.

Sheriff Martin peered over the edge again; it was a thousand feet straight down onto the jagged rocks below.

"Ropes," she mumbled. "We don't need ropes, we need wings."

Logan snapped the slack out of his line, stepped to the edge of the cliff face and leaned forward. Glancing back at Raven, he nodded, and then stepped off over the cliff.

"Time to fly!"

Chapter 37: Here We Go

As Logan rappelled down the cliff, a gust of wind pounded him against the rocks so hard he had to grab a handhold and hang on for dear life. Scrambling over the icy boulders, he eventually landed on a narrow ledge of the trail that led along the rock face to the opening of the cave.

"You're next!" Logan shouted up to Billie Sue, reeling in his line against the rocks.

"Me?" Sheriff Martin begged Raven.

"Don't worry, I've got you," Raven assured her, as she tied the harness around her waist, pulling it taut.

"I'm not sure I'm meant to fly."

"Spread your wings, Sheriff. Now go!"

Billie Sue took a deep breath and eased timidly over the edge, bouncing hesitantly down the rock face. Despite both Raven and Logan anchoring their support lines firm, Sheriff Martin still managed to crash against the rocks several times. As she reached the end of the rope, Logan was waiting on the ledge.

"That wasn't so bad, was it?" he assured her as he grabbed the harness, clamped his tie down, and balanced her on the ledge.

"Piece of cake. Let's go again!" Billie Sue managed, kneeling down to rub the growing knot on her knee.

Logan snapped the rope to signal Raven and then bent down to examine Sheriff Martin's injury.

"That doesn't look so bad," Raven assessed as she leaned around Logan and poked the sheriff's knee. "I can wrap a bandage on it if you want."

Billie Sue glanced at Raven, then up the rock face,

and then back at Raven. "How did you get down here so fast?"

"I saw the wind knocking you around, so I took another route."

"Another route?"

"On wings of eagles, Sheriff. Let's go."

Raven quickly secured the ropes and led the three of them along the narrow trail until they came to a small cairn on a broad stone ledge covered with gnarled evergreens at the mouth of the cave.

Logan held up his hand and paused as he observed a circle of smooth stones on the ledge outside the cave. The stones formed an old fire ring that was perched at the edge of the cliff. The first time he and Raven had entered this cave, he hadn't noticed the charred aspen logs or the fire ring guarding the entrance. He wouldn't make that mistake again. As he bent down and touched the smooth stones, his mind flashed back to an old lesson from Ten Bears: *"Select a large, smooth stone that parts the river,"* Ten Bears had said. *"One that has forced the current to bend. These are the stones that understand both conflict, and patience."*

Following Ten Bears' instructions, he'd lugged those stones from the riverbed up Wuutaqa Mountain, carefully placing them in the fire ring. Patiently, he stood there in the rain for hours, arms extended skyward, asking the Thunder Gods to smile upon him, but nothing happened.

"When you are worthy," Ten Bears had reassured him, "they will come."

"Are you OK?" Raven nudged, interrupting Logan's dream state.

Logan shook his head and snapped back to the moment. Instinctively, he reached inside his jacket and clutched the medicine bag around his neck, carefully removing a shell, a feather, and a small pinch of white sage. He packed the sage into the shell, lit it on fire, and used the feather to swirl a small puff of smoke around his face. As the smoke purified his thoughts, Logan closed his eyes, opened his mind, and paid homage to the Ancient Ones. "I am now," Logan opened his eyes. "Let's go."

Just inside the cave, they dropped their packs as Raven rummaged in the bushes until she dug out an old wooden torch and lit it from the ember still burning in Logan's shell.

"Come on," she said, waving the flame. "I can't keep this going out here in the wind!"

Inside the cave, Raven guided the search party along a rocky crevice until the trail opened up into a large, circular hollow. Logan found another torch, lit it, and the flickering light scattered across the ceiling to reveal a vast tapestry of Native American petroglyphs and rock paintings. The images were well preserved, untouched for centuries, and they were stunning.

There were men on horseback with bows and arrows chasing buffalo across the plains. Across the wall was a giant mountain, a waterfall, and a raging river that cascaded down from the highest peaks into a cave, terminating into a large dark pool. At the peak of the roof, there were many brightly colored iconic symbols. Clustered in the center of the ceiling, there were massive storm clouds and lightning bolts. Beneath the clouds was an old rope bridge across the dark pool with a single figure standing in the middle of the bridge, holding a spear, and wearing a death mask.

"What does all this mean?" Sheriff Martin asked.

"It means we've crossed the boundary to the Rez,

and this a sacred place," Raven began.

"A place where we shouldn't be," Logan shuddered. "A place that can never be revealed. Come on, we're almost there."

Taking the lead, Logan waved his torch and followed the rocky trail deeper into the mountain, descending through several caverns until he could hear the faint sound of running water. "We're here!" Logan exclaimed as he climbed on top of a boulder, pointing his torch at an old rope bridge that spanned a dark pool of still water.

On one side of the pool, there was a fissure in the rocks beneath the roof of the cavern where a stream bubbled over a rocky ledge, dripping down into the dark pool. At the other end of the still water, a waterfall cascaded over jagged rocks, down into the darkness, and deep inside the mountain. The drop of the waterfall at the end of the pool was an abyss with the sound of the water splashing far below, creating a faint echo reverberating inside the cavern.

"What *is* this place?" Sheriff Martin whispered.

"Our people know it as the River of Lost Souls," Raven lectured, pointing into the abyss. "A place not to be remembered, and a place not to be spoken of...unless you want to go over the falls."

Logan started across the old rope bridge and then hesitated in the middle, closing his eyes. He winced as he nearly was overwhelmed by the impassioned cries and pleas for help that surged through his mind. The voices of human skeletons screamed out to him from the darkened crevices of the cave, sending a shiver down his spine, and then dissipated into silence when he opened his eyes.

"Come on," Logan said softly, shaking his head.

He pointed his torch across the rope bridge. "We must not linger here; cross over to the other side."

"What's on the other side?" Billie Sue asked, wide-eyed.

"If we're lucky, Sheriff, our lost girl."

"And if we're not lucky?"

"Let's just hope we're lucky."

Balancing with one hand on the rope bridge and the other on his torch, Logan crossed over the pool and led the party along the trail to a waterfall flowing from the ceiling. Beneath the waterfall, he paused, sniffed the air, and then motioned for Raven and the sheriff to follow. Once the others joined him, Logan silently proceeded behind the waterfall and into another passageway. Beyond the cascading water was an opening that led into a large cavern, and beyond it, a labyrinth of tunnels that led deeper into the pitch darkness.

At the far side of the cavern, Logan squinted his eyes, as he barely could make out the flickering light of a campfire surrounded by smooth boulders.

Logan froze. He cocked his head and listened for a moment in silence. Watching patiently, he observed as the shadows of the fire danced erratically across the cavern ceiling, until finally, he heard a sound.

It was the muffled sob of a young girl.

"I think we've found them," Logan whispered, pointing at the boulders. "Up ahead, behind those rocks."

Raven and Sheriff Martin held their breath until the sound of the girl's sobbing returned, sadly echoing throughout the cavern.

"OK, let's take this slow," Billie Sue cautioned as she drew her gun, checked the magazine, and stepped in front of Logan. "Slow and easy."

.

Chapter 38: Deep Discovery

Sheriff Martin crept silently across the cave toward the sound of the sobbing girl. When she reached the boulders near the fire, she leaned around one and peered over. There, sitting next to the smoldering embers of the campfire, was the ranger imposter, holding the girl. The escaped mental patient fiddled with her handgun, softly stroked the hair of the sobbing girl lying on her lap, and then poked the fire.

"There, there," the mental patient whispered in the girl's ear. "Just relax. It will all be over soon."

Billie Sue glanced over at Logan on the other side of the fire behind a boulder, and motioned for him to stay put. She slowly stood up, leveled her weapon at the woman, and cleared her throat.

Without looking up, the woman instinctively tightened her grip on the girl's hair and aimed her gun in the direction of the noise in the shadows.

"Hello, Sheriff," the woman said calmly. "Once again, you're late to the party. What brings you up here to my little slice of paradise?"

Billie Sue stepped into the light of the fire, keeping her weapon trained on the imposter. "The new intern over at park headquarters said you were out tracking down poachers," Sheriff Martin said. "I was in the neighborhood, so I thought I'd see if you needed any help."

"Well, that is mighty neighborly of you, Sheriff, but no, I'm good," the woman laughed as she stood up, dragging the frightened girl with her by the hair.

Billie Sue peered across the iridescent firelight of

the campfire, trying to see if the girl had been harmed.

"One step closer, Sheriff, and we'll have another homecoming, minus a queen."

"OK, OK," Billie Sue hesitated. "Just take it easy."

"Stay where you are, or I'll part Queeny's baby blues with a bullet. You don't want to spoil her prom dress, do you?"

The girl squirmed for a second and then fell limp with fear.

"I think the pretty ones like to know what's coming, don't you, Sheriff?" the woman said, as she rubbed the gun across the terrified girl's temple, down her forehead, and then trained the weapon on the sheriff.

"It's kind of a control thing; the pretty ones always have to be in control." The imposter glanced down at the reflection of fear in the girl's eyes. "I know I would...like to see it coming, that is. I don't like surprises. Surprises can be deadly."

Sheriff Martin remained still.

"No surprises here," Billie Sue said as she lowered her weapon. "Let's all stay calm here."

Logan slowly stepped out from behind a boulder, looked at the woman, and then again to Billie Sue for how to play the confrontation.

"Drop the gun, Sheriff," the mental patient demanded. "Now!"

"OK," Billie Sue nodded and slowly set her pistol on the ground.

"Now, kick it over here."

Sheriff Martin complied.

The fake ranger looked at Logan in the flickering light, studying his face.

"You? It's Logan, right?" the woman said. "Toss

your torch into the fire. It's not good to play with matches, you know."

"Let the girl go," Billie Sue insisted, "and no one has to get hurt."

"Now, why would I want to do that?"

"We know about your…sickness; we'll see that you get the help you need."

"It's the end of the trail," Logan interrupted. "You need to let her go."

The mental patient examined Logan's face in the firelight and smiled. "The end of the trail? You know it's not the end, don't you?"

"It doesn't have to be if you let her go," Logan answered, moving one step closer.

"No, it's not the end," the woman smiled, "it's just the beginning."

Sheriff Martin glanced at Logan; she was confused.

"I knew you would come," the woman continued, glaring at Logan. "Ten years…That's a long time for us to wait."

"It is a long time," Logan responded, as he nudged closer to the fire between him and the fake ranger. He studied her face, took a deep breath, and defocused his eyes.

As Logan exhaled, his mind entered a dream state. His vision was blurry for a moment, and then he could feel the emotional torment of the woman's past. Strangely, it was the same anguish that he'd endured in his dreams for the last ten years. There was a subliminal voice, taunting her, commanding her to do things she didn't want to do. She tried to resist, but it was too late; the voice had grown strong. Logan felt a knot in his stomach and almost vomited, the convulsions snapped him back to reality.

"It doesn't have to be that way," he gagged, still sick to his stomach.

"What way?"

"The way he wants it to be."

"What would you know about that?" the woman asked smugly.

"I know about him, what he says. Trust me, I know."

"He said you would say that, try and trick me, just like my therapist did. 'Just trust me,' he said. 'Tell me what's in your head...Nothing bad will happen.' Well, when I told him the truth and exposed his lies, he got a little surprise for his deception, he did. Lots of people have deceived me. Most of them are dead."

"Your therapist is alive," Sheriff Martin interrupted. "I talked to him today."

"No, he's not," the woman snapped back. "He's dead; I made him go away. Now you're lying to me, too."

"I know what you see when you close your eyes," Logan interrupted. "I know why you're afraid to go to sleep at night."

"What?" the woman exclaimed. "You don't know anything about what it's like!"

"I know about the weight you carry, about the guilt. He tells you that you have no choice, but you do. You can choose to lay your burden down, right here, right now, and you can walk away from this. You can walk away...from him."

"He says you know nothing, except about your guilt! You're the guilty one."

"Listen to me, Sharon, not to him."

The woman glanced at Logan with a look of suspicion. "How do you know my name? Ah, he told you. You hear him too, don't you? The voice, I mean."

"Yes," Logan hesitated. "I do."

"Then it's true what he says…You and me, we're both part of the grand play."

"A play is just a script," Logan countered. "It's a one-dimensional story with a predetermined ending. But you and me, Sharon, we're the actors; we're alive. We can change the script and control how the play ends."

"Control it?" Sharon screamed. "I couldn't control it ten years ago, and I can't control it now!"

"I believe you can—*we* can."

"No, I can't control it," Sharon lamented. "This is beyond the point of no return. You know that it is."

Sharon closed her eyes, shook her head, and called out to the darkness of cave. "I did what you asked!" she shouted. "I brought the girl here, and he came for her, just like you said he would. I've played my part!"

Logan stepped forward, but suddenly Sharon opened her eyes and shoved the gun to the girl's forehead, causing him to stop. She tightened her grip on the girl.

"Stop it! Please!" the girl cried out in pain.

"Come and take them," Sharon sobbed. "Set me free, like you promised!"

Suddenly, there was a deep growl from a dark part of the cave, the huffing sound of a giant bear, and then a nasty, putrid smell.

Logan had smelled this smell before, at Spirit Lake, at Wapiti Meadows, in the landfill…and in this cave, ten years ago.

He recognized the rancid smell; it was the smell of death.

Chapter 39: Bear Aware

From the darkness of the cave, the sound of the angry bear grew louder. It was stomping the ground, ready to charge.

Logan locked his eyes on Sharon, at the same time motioning to Raven with his hand behind his back. Raven emerged from the behind the boulder and joined Logan, standing just in back of him in the darkness.

"No matter what happens," he whispered to Raven, "you stay with the sheriff and the girl."

"Why?" Raven protested.

"To protect them from what's coming. It's time to finish what I started," Logan said softly as he removed his jacket. "When the fire goes out, grab the girl and get out of here."

"Not this time, Niwot." Raven looked at Logan, pleading with her eyes. "Ten Bears said we must stay together."

"Yes, he did. And we are together...for now." Logan turned to Raven and looked deep into her eyes. "I have never told you this, but we've always been together in my heart, and we always will be. But what is here in the dark, what I unleashed ten years ago, I must face it alone."

"No!" Raven insisted.

Logan reached inside his shirt and clutched his medicine bag. In one swift move, he tossed his jacket over the fire, stamped on it, and smothered out the flames. The cavern quickly filled with a smoky haze; coughs, screams, and the roar of a ferocious bear in the darkness echoed throughout the cavern. In the midst of the chaos around him, Logan defocused his eyes and slipped into a dream state.

From the far side of the darkness, he heard a deep growl, and then the terrifying sound of the giant bear charging across the cave floor at full speed.

Chapter 40: Shared Vision

In the pitch black of the smoky cave, Logan could see through the eyes of the giant bear as it closed in on Sharon. The animal reared up on its hind legs and snarled, drool dripping over its enormous fangs. Leaning down to within inches of the woman's head, the bear slowly opened its mouth and growled.

Trembling, Sharon brought her gun to her side and faced the bear; it was the giant cinnamon-colored killer of her nightmares. "I've done what you asked!" Sharon pleaded, the gun in her hand shaking. "Now...Do as you promised!"

The bear snarled, flexed its paw, and raked Sharon's arm with its razor-sharp claws, knocking her to the ground. As her arm spewed blood from the ragged gash, Sharon struggled to one knee while still clutching her screaming captive by her hair.

"Why?" Sharon begged.

"Because you are weak!" the bear called out from its mind. "You are worthless to me now, or anyone else!"

As the bear lunged forward, a single shot rang out, penetrating the giant bear's front leg point-blank as it clamped its jaws on Sharon Summerhill's throat. The bear shuddered in pain from the forty-five-caliber wound, tossing Sharon and the girl in her arms against the wall of the cave, knocking them both unconscious.

With a mighty roar, the enormous bear licked the blood seeping out from its wounded leg and then slowly turned around, sniffing the smoky air. The beast cocked its head and quickly located Logan's scent in the darkness. "Yes, there you are…" the bear turned its head.

Logan remained silent, flush against the wall of the cave.

"You can't hide from me now," the bear taunted as it flared its nostrils. "I can smell your fear."

Chapter 41: Death Mask

"You can't hide from your past," the bear snarled as it scanned the darkness of the cave, detecting a faint silhouette through the smoldering embers of the campfire. "Ah yes, there you are."

Logan shook his head and tried to snap out of his dream state; the images of the cave remained fuzzy for a moment. He scanned the cavern; there, against the wall, was the missing girl lying under the body of the unconscious ranger. Raven and Sheriff Martin had taken shelter behind a boulder in the darkness, but they were frozen in place, still unable to see. It was as if time had been suspended and Logan was alone in the darkness of the cave, facing the evil from his own tormented dreams.

"If this is all about you and me," Logan said, moving silently away from the wall, "why all the drama? I answered your call. You didn't need the others. I would have come anyway."

He stepped past the fire, away from Raven, toward the labyrinth of tunnels by the dark pool.

The bear sniffed the air and snarled, trying to track his movements, but the faint silhouette faded in and out of his vision. "The others," the bear's voice said in his mind. "They were just part of the grand bargain—collateral, you might say."

Logan continued walking backwards while facing the bear as it tracked him, making his way toward the dark pool of still water.

"I called to you," the bear taunted, "many times in your dreams."

"Uninvited, I might add," Logan countered. "But yes, I heard you."

"You found my voice disturbing, and yet you returned to this place. Interesting."

"Yes, I did."

"Why did you return?"

Logan stopped and clutched his medicine bag. "You know why I came back."

"And why is that, Lone Bear?"

"I came back to end this nightmare. I came back...to kill you."

"To kill me?" the bear laughed. "You've got it backwards, my little friend. You didn't come here to kill me, you came here to kill yourself. You came here to die."

The smoke parted and Logan could see Sharon's body now in the faint light of the smoldering fire, lying against the wall. "Then why did you have to kill this woman? She said she did as you asked. Are the words of a powerful spirit just lies?"

The bear snarled.

"She was just a tool, as are all from your world. Except for the old one who stands in the path. He is different."

"You mean Ten Bears?"

"Yes, Ten Bears, as you call him. Where is he now? I think he must be hiding in his sweat lodge, conjuring up some more of his bad medicine. I think he is not here because he has abandoned you. But then again, he has done that before, has he not? Abandoned you, that is, just like everyone else in your world."

Logan rubbed the medicine bag around his neck and took a deep breath. "No, he's here. Ten Bears is with me."

"The old one does not matter anyway; he is nearly finished. Soon, the path will be clear."

"The path will be clear...for what?"

"For breaking the Covenant."

Logan stepped back, continuing to lead the bear away from the others. "The Covenant? I don't know what you are talking about."

The bear stopped and studied Logan's face in the smoky haze.

"You know of what I speak, Lone Bear, the bridge that separates your world from ours. The Covenant is the reason that it exists."

"Come to think of it, I do remember something about that. Ten Bears babbled on about it one night, but I always thought it was just another of the old man's tales, more of his bad medicine."

The bear looked deep into Logan's eyes. He sniffed the air and studied the medicine bag around his neck, sensing the contents of the bag. "I see now...You think you have the power, very clever, but very foolish. The old one has convinced you that you can wield his medicine."

"Medicine? That's what all that gibberish was? If I'd known that, I probably would have paid more attention to his ramblings. You think I have some kind of powers?"

"It will never come to pass," the bear taunted, shaking his head. "The old one will soon join his ancestors, and you are not worthy to take his place."

"Hey, I don't want to take anyone's place," Logan said, stepping back again.

"Why are you stalling, Lone Bear?" The bear stopped and turned around, focusing on Raven and Sheriff Martin, frozen in place on the other side of the cavern. "Oh, I see, your little friends. They think they can rescue the girl. They do not appear to be going anywhere, so I will deal with them soon enough. It is time."

"Wait, before I go, there's something I must know."

"A last request?"

"Even a condemned man gets a last request."

"Make it quick, as you are stretching my patience."

"You're a bear," Logan mocked. "And a powerful one, I might add. But you're not like any bear I know."

"What would you know of who I am?"

"I think you're pretending to be a Nanulak, a mythical cross between a grizzly and a polar bear. Is that how you lure them in? The thrill of discovery?"

"The discovery of what?"

"The discovery of something…unknown. A real Nanulak, known only in Native American legends. It is a great and powerful creature, so my Inuit brothers say."

The bear laughed. "Your kind only sees what you want to believe. That is what I tell them in their minds." The bear cocked its head again, sniffing Logan. "You are different somehow from when we last met: smarter…more devious, but that is of little consequence."

"I think you're masquerading as a Nanulak," Logan taunted, "the legendary bear from the north. But really, you're neither a bear nor a Nanulak, are you?"

The bear snarled and opened its jaws.

"I know who you really are, *Niatha*. You showed me your true face a long time ago."

The bear huffed and stood on its hind legs, growling with hot, wet drool dripping down its fangs.

"The unworthy one, the one who dares to say my name, you are nothing but a thief. You stole something from me the last time we met, didn't you? Something that does not belong to you."

"Not anything I wanted, I can assure you."

"Nonetheless, you have it now, don't you?"

"I don't know what you mean."

"Yes, you do. I see it now; you have the power, but you don't know how to use it. You have stumbled onto the power to enter my world, but through your eyes, foolish one, now I can enter your world as well."

"You can't enter my world; you haven't been invited. That would break your sacred Covenant."

"Ah ha! You do know of the Covenant. Then you also know that I can cross the bridge between worlds once I have been invited."

"Well, that's not going to happen, even if you kill me."

"You forget, clever one, I have already been invited."

"When? By who?"

"Ten years ago…by you, foolish one."

Logan's vision grew cloudy and his mind spun uncontrollably into a dream. It was ten years ago; he was in the cave, playing with Raven. The bear came for her, to kill her. Logan shoved her aside to protect her and shouted at the bear to distract it.

"Chase me!" Logan screamed, taunting the bear. He ran, the bear chased him, and he climbed the bridge over the dark pool.

"Come on, follow me!" Logan invited. The bear lunged and caught him by the leg on the bridge, raking its claws across his chest. Logan fell to his knees, blood oozing from the gaping wound in his chest. He gripped the rope bridge; the pain was unbearable, and his mind spun a dream to block the agony.

In Logan's mind, he was flying on the back of a giant bird, up and away from the bear, away from the ache in his chest. He could see above the clouds; they were floating on air, and it was beautiful. But then, suddenly, he lost his grip on the giant bird and plunged back down to earth, into the cave, into the cold dark pool of water beneath the bridge.

There was a flash of light, and Logan's dream world of the past dissolved. He was once again back in the cave, standing on the rope bridge alone and facing the bear, just as he had ten years ago.

"Maybe you're right," Logan said as the bear pursued him onto the rope bridge. "Maybe it was me that opened the door and let you into our world."

The bear reared up on its hind legs, ready to strike.

"Or maybe that was a dream long ago, maybe you've always been a dream. Either way, that reality is over for me now; that dream must come to an end."

Logan clutched the medicine bag around his neck, stood tall in the center of the rope bridge, and faced the Shadow Bear. "It is finished for you and me. Today is a good day to die."

Chapter 42: Unresolved Questions

Inside the cave, Sheriff Martin groped around in the darkness until she found one of the snuffed-out torches lying next to the campfire. Relighting it, she discovered the unconscious mental patient crumpled against the wall of the cave, smoking gun in hand, with the missing girl underneath her. She rolled Sharon off the dazed girl and untied her, examining the gaping wound on Sharon's throat. Blood was splattered everywhere. The lacerations were deep, down to the carotid artery. She ripped off one of her shirtsleeves and wrapped it around the woman's neck, trying to slow down the bleeding.

"My throat," Sharon moaned as she fought to regain consciousness.

"Don't move, I bandaged your wound, but you have to lie still or you'll start the bleeding again."

"Where am I?" the missing girl rubbed her forehead as she regained consciousness.

"Are you OK?" Sheriff Martin turned around and asked the confused girl.

"I think so…everything is…spinning. I must have hit my head on a rock."

"You're all right. Sit there for a minute and focus on the campfire. Don't close your eyes—that will make it worse."

Sharon Summerhill reached up and felt the throbbing gash on her neck and looked down at her blood-soaked clothes. "Am I going to die?" she asked, still woozy from the trauma.

"You've got one nasty bite on your neck," Sheriff

Martin said as she tried to remain positive, "but you'll make it; I've seen worse. We need to get you to a hospital."

"I'm going to die here, alone."

"No, you're not alone, Sharon. I won't leave you. As soon as Caroline over there can walk, we're all getting out of here.

"Thank you, Sheriff," the ranger imposter exhaled as she sagged back against the rocks, seeming to forget for a moment her part in the current situation.

Billie Sue knew that despite the immediate need for medical attention, neither of the girls were going anywhere for now. She tried to make them comfortable, all the while replaying in her mind the twisted path that had guided them here. How those events had caused an escaped mental patient to kidnap an innocent girl and lead them to this remote mountain cave was clear; the question was *why*?

"You know," Sheriff Martin turned back to Sharon Summerhill, "in all the confusion, there's still a couple of things nagging at me in the back of my head. It's like pieces of a puzzle that are missing."

Sharon closed her eyes and slumped over. "I hate puzzles."

"I do too," Sheriff Martin continued. "Until they are put back together and placed neatly in the box. Are you still with me?"

"Yes, I'm listening," Sharon responded without opening her eyes.

"The nine millimeter that was used to kill the boy," Billie Sue began, "how did it end up on the outlaw? I'm stumped."

"Really, Sheriff? With all we've been through together, that's what is bothering you?"

"I'm a creature of habit. Humor me."

"Alright, we were searching the torn backpack in the campground at Spirit Lake before you interrupted us with your *wildlife-related* incident. The nine was just lying there, so I pocketed it. You never know when you might need a throwaway."

"A throwaway?"

"Come on, Sheriff, I've seen your drop gun. You carry one when you need a little *nudge* to close a case, don't you?"

"Back to my question. How did the nine millimeter end up on the outlaw?"

"A slight of hand, like your throwaway. I dropped the gun in the outlaw's backpack when you captured him at Wolf Creek."

"And that's the gun you used to murder the boy in Wapiti Meadows, right?"

"If you say so, Sheriff. It's all a little hazy to me now."

"Hazy or not, I'm afraid you're going in for that one, Sharon. We found your DNA."

"Prison? I'll never see the inside of a cell, and you know it. I'm a disturbed mental patient; I need help, not incarceration."

"What about your DNA on the murder weapon?"

"Come on, Sheriff, forensic evidence like DNA can be faked as easily as changing your identity. You and I know that people aren't who they appear to be, not on this mountain, and not in Austin."

"What do you know about Austin?"

"Me? Nothing really, I'm just an insignificant cog in the wheel of the universe. But this I do know, Sheriff, we've both got skeletons buried in our past. And that's the thing about skeletons, no matter how far you run, they always catch up to you."

"You've lost a lot of blood; maybe you should rest now."

"'If you sit by a river long enough, you'll see the bodies of your enemies float by,'" Sharon laughed, "that's what they told me."

"What does that mean?"

The ranger imposter opened her eyes and smiled. "It means that they know what you've done, and they know what you'll do when the time comes. We all have to pay for our sins in this life."

The ranger imposter slumped down, winced, and closed her eyes. "I couldn't run from my past any more than you can hide from yours," Sharon Summerhill mumbled. "When the dead reveal their secrets, your marker gets called. The darkness always claims his due, Sheriff; no escaping that. Now, my head is spinning...I need to rest."

"Wait, just one more question," Billie Sue redirected, "the funeral director. He said that you picked up a dead body from him three weeks ago."

"That seems...right," Sharon muttered. "What of it?"

"He said you didn't pay for the body; someone else did."

"I guess so. I didn't have any money."

"But *who* did that? Paid for the body, I mean?"

Sharon slowly opened her eyes for a moment, struggling to remain conscious. "Someone above your pay grade, Sheriff."

"Do you have a name?"

"I never had a name, just a phone number."

"What is it?"

"I don't remember," Sharon closed her eyes again.

"But I wrote it on my hand."

Chapter 43: Volte-Face

"Sheriff?" Caroline's frightened voice echoed in the cave as she tried to stand. "I want to go home."

Billie Sue stood and put her arm around the wobbly girl, trying to prop her up.

"If you can walk, we'll all try to go home. Let's get you two out of here."

As Sheriff Martin steadied the dazed girl, she turned around to offer her other hand to Sharon Summerhill, only to find herself staring down the barrel of a forty-five-caliber Glock.

"We're not leaving just yet," Sharon proclaimed. "We've got some…unfinished business."

"Really? You think killing me is a good idea right now?"

"I'm afraid so, Sheriff."

"Why are you hell-bent to have this end badly?" Billie Sue pushed the kidnapped girl behind her.

"It all has to end sometime," Sharon smiled.

"If you shoot me, you're never going to make it off this mountain alive."

"No matter what I do," Sharon grew somber, "none of us are going to make it off this mountain alive."

Sharon paused, and Billie Sue thought she could see a hint of sadness in her eyes. But before she could speak, the ranger imposter rammed the Glock into her mouth and pulled the trigger.

Bang!

Chapter 44: Metamorphosis

Logan's mind screamed as the giant Shadow Bear chased him, shaking his balance on the rope bridge. The bear swiped at his legs, opened its jaws, and prepared to deliver its deathblow. In Logan's mind, voices shouted out in the swirling chaos of the moment.

"The ranger's bullet didn't slow the beast down."

"'You can control your destiny."

"We either hang together, or we'll hang separately."

"If the bear is not a bear, then to kill it, you cannot be a man."

Logan took a deep breath, closed his eyes, and immediately was transported into his dream world. Through the swirling haze in his mind, Raven appeared. A moment ago, she had been frozen in place, across the cave, and now she was standing just behind him.

"We must stay together," Raven whispered.

"This is my fight!"

"It is *our* fight!" Raven corrected him. "Use what Ten Bears has taught you, *yee naaldlooshii!*"

Raven's image dissolved in a gust of beating wings as the smoke cleared in front of him. As Logan looked up in the darkness, the winged sound in the darkness spiraled skyward outside the cave, and then faded into the clouds. He grabbed the side of the wobbly rope bridge and stood, defiantly facing the Shadow Bear. "You want me?" Logan screamed. "Then you will know my name!"

"Neneeni-noo Nowoo3! Nenééninoo hoowóóh híis hiihooteet, Nih'oo3oo, neneeni-noo wóóukohéi hiihooteet! I am

Niwot! I no longer fear death, Niatha, I welcome death!"

Suddenly, in a flash of light, there were two bears balanced on the rope bridge—a Nanulak and a grizzly. They reared up on their hind legs and swiped at each other with their front claws, ripping mounds of flesh as they thrashed about for dominance.

"Now I can see your true face as well. Finally, a soul worthy of taking!" the Nanulak snarled, raking its claws across the grizzly's chest. "Your spirit is mine, Niwot!"

With a mighty thrust, the Nanulak clamped its jaws on the grizzly's neck, shook him violently, and tossed him through the air. Badly wounded, the grizzly landed on the other side of the rope bridge, barely able to move. The Nanulak slowly crossed over the bridge, hovering above the injured grizzly.

"At first, I was just a weak voice inside you," the Nanulak taunted, looking back at the cave. "But each day that you doubted yourself, each day that you felt worthless, I grew stronger. Now it is you that is weak, and I that am strong. You are right, Niwot, it is the end of the dream. And in the end, there can be only one voice."

The wounded grizzly desperately crawled out from under the Nanulak toward the opening of the cave and collapsed next to the charred fire ring. Weak and bleeding badly, Logan slipped in and out of his dream state. He felt the cool, smooth stones against his face, and somehow through the pain, he managed to drag the broken body of the grizzly into the center of the fire ring.

"Bring down your thunder from the sky," Logan began to chant.

"The Ancient Ones can't hear you," the Nanulak mocked as it approached.

"And purify my soul," the grizzly chanted louder, looking skyward.

"And the Old One can't save you this time."

Battered and bloody, the grizzly hunched on one knee, and then wobbled to stand on its hind legs in the center of the fire ring. The clouds darkened as the wind swirled above the ledge.

"Your soul is mine!" the Nanulak screamed.

"My soul?" the grizzly screamed back, raising its front legs into the snowy sky, singing its death song. "My soul will be purified..."

"The Old One hides in his crazy lodge," the Nanulak laughed. "And your little friend has flown away. Again, they have abandoned you. It is time."

Above the rocky ledge, the darkened clouds swirled as a violent windstorm gathered.

"No one has heard your death song!" the Nanulak taunted as it lunged on the grizzly to end its life. "You are finished!"

Just as the Nanulak delivered its deathblow, the mountain shook with an enormous clap of thunder. Above the fire ring, rapidly spinning clouds parted, and a hole opened in the dark sky. There was an ear-piercing screech as the silhouette of a giant bird swooped down from the heavens, launching the three lightning bolts clutched in its talons. On the rocky ledge, it was pandemonium: an explosion, blood-curling shrieks of pain, and a huge ball of flames exploding upwards into the sky. The fire ring was engulfed in smoke with the lingering smell of charred flesh.

And then, there was silence.

Chapter 45: Burning Flesh

As the flames of burning flesh licked high above the rocky ledge at the entrance to the cave, smoke filled the air, heavy with the choking smell of singed hair and skin. Hovering above the mayhem, a giant white owl circled and flapped its wings, slowly causing the smoke to part.

From the murky haze, Raven leapt atop a boulder beside the fire ring, terrified at what she might discover. "Niwot!" she screamed. "Where are you?"

In the center of the fire ring, there was nothing but the burned carcass of the Nanulak, still smoldering in the ashes.

"No!" Raven sobbed, falling to her knees. "No…"

She buried her face in her hands and tears ran down her cheeks, dripping onto the hot stones of the fire ring with a hiss. As the steam rose from the stones, there was a brief, convulsive movement from the body of the Nanulak, and then it collapsed motionless in the fire ring.

"Logan!" Raven screamed, her voice echoing through the cave.

The echoes faded into silence; there was no answer.

"Niwot," she whispered as she placed her hand over her heart. Raven knelt there with her eyes closed for what seemed an eternity, remembering his face, the touch of his hand, and her last words to Logan.

"I told you not to leave me!" she scolded, standing to stomp the ground as she wiped a tear from her eye. Just as she stepped away from the fire ring, the remains of the charred bear disintegrated into ashes, leaving only an outline of the beast that had attacked them in the sacred cave.

And then, as Raven stared up at the sky in sorrow, something unexpected happened. A gust of wind stirred the pile of ashes, exposing a human hand protruding from the center of the fire ring.

"Logan?" Raven shouted, reaching down to grasp the blackened fingers from under the debris. She pulled on the quivering hand, wrenching a disheveled Logan from the mound of smoldering remains in the pit.

Logan coughed, brushed some of the soot and burnt flesh from his body, and then smiled, unable to speak.

"I thought I'd lost you," Raven sniffed as she hugged Logan. "Don't you ever leave me again!"

"I won't," Logan exhaled, still gasping for air.

"You better not!" Raven cocked her head and smiled. "Or next time, I'll kill you myself."

Chapter 46: Forbidden Ground

The sharp reverberation of a gunshot ricocheted through the cavern, penetrating deep into the tunnels inside the mountain. Finally, when the last muffled echo died away, Sheriff Martin slowly opened her eyes. She shook her head and carefully wiped away some of the blood splatter covering her face and shirt. "Damn it! After all this, why did you have to go and do that?"

From behind her, Billie Sue could feel the kidnapped girl clutching her leg and trembling. "You OK?" the sheriff asked, turning around.

"I'm OK."

"Can you walk now?"

"I think so."

"Good. Let's get out of here."

With one arm around the shaky girl and the other holding a torch, Sheriff Martin made her way out of the cavern, across the rope bridge, and started up the rocky trail leading from the cave. At the cave's entrance, there was a lingering haze, but through the smoke she could make out the silhouette of a figure standing just outside on the ledge. The smoke cleared, and there was Logan, charred, and much to her surprise, quite alive.

"Well you are a sight for sore eyes!" Billie Sue exclaimed, scanning Logan's burned clothing before giving him a hug. "When the lights went out in there, I wasn't sure if I'd ever see you again."

"Me?" Logan laughed, glancing at the sheriff's blood-splattered face and shirt. "You were the one I was worried about."

"Well, looks like we survived, and Caroline here's

going to be all right as well."

"I take it Sharon didn't?" Logan inquired, glancing back into the cave.

"No, she didn't."

"I was afraid of that. Her therapist said she was borderline comatose for years; she finally comes out of it and then something snaps."

"I know—weird."

"I tried to pull her back from the edge, but I couldn't reach her."

"Some people," Sheriff Martin tried to comfort Logan, "you just can't reach. There's no explanation, she was just one sick puppy, if you ask me."

"I guess."

"Speaking of explaining things," Billie Sue switched gears, looking at the outline of the burnt carcass in the fire ring, "what the hell was that?"

"That was the bear we've been chasing, Sheriff."

"The man-eater? I never want to see that son of a bitch again."

"Me neither, Sheriff."

"What kind of bear do you think that was?"

"It was a Nanulak," Raven spoke up, emerging from the haze.

"A what?"

"A Nanulak," Logan responded. "A cross between a polar bear and a grizzly. It's a carnivore; doesn't hibernate. That's why it was out raising hell in the middle of winter."

Sheriff Martin walked around the fire ring, studying the charred remains.

"So that's all that's left of our man-eater?"

"Seems to be."

"What was it doing all the way down here? In

Colorado, I mean?"

"I don't know, Sheriff." Logan stood on the edge of the rocks and looked out across the Continental Divide, "The Ancient Ones say that all things are connected. When you pull a strand on the web of life, there are unintended consequences."

"Really," Billie Sue pondered, looking at Logan and then back to Raven. "Polar bears moving down from the Arctic, munching on the locals? Didn't see that one coming."

"When you think about it," Logan thought aloud, "it's inevitable, really."

"Inevitable…" Sheriff Martin walked back to the fire ring, studying the ashes. "And that's all that's left of it? A Nanulak, you called it?"

"Yes."

"What the hell did you two do to him?"

Logan stepped back from the ledge and joined Raven and Billie Sue, staring down at the outline of the charred remains. "We had kind of a…*bear*beque."

"That's it?" Sheriff Martin puzzled, waiting for a more plausible explanation.

"That's it."

"Yeah, OK, a Cajun *bear*beque. Burnt to a crisp. If you ask me, looks like he's a little overdone for my taste."

Billie Sue started to press her questioning further, but decided it was neither the time nor the place for a long interrogation. "I guess I should at least gather some evidence," Sheriff Martin said, as she bent down to collect a handful of bear ashes in a plastic bag.

"No!" Raven shouted, grabbing her hand and pulling the sheriff away from the fire ring. "No one can touch those ashes."

"Why?" Billie Sue asked.

"It is forbidden."

Before Sheriff Martin's confusion could manifest itself into another question, there was an intense thunderclap in the sky above them. The clouds parted for a moment, and a swirling gust engulfed the ledge, sucking the ashes from the fire ring upward into a whirlwind, and then back into the cave.

Chapter 47: Small Victories

Sheriff Martin stared up at the darkened sky along the Continental Divide. Looking back into the cave, she was unsure how to comprehend what she'd just witnessed. Standing on that rocky ledge, the ashes of the man-eating bear in the fire ring were gone, leaving no trace that it ever had been there at all. She started to speak, but before she could formulate a question, Logan put his hand on her shoulder. "We should go now."

"This is no place to linger," Raven added, retrieving their packs from the bushes near the cave entrance.

Sheriff Martin slipped on her pack, still trying to process what just had happened. "Seems that this crime spree was ten years in the making," Billie Sue said, as she tried to reach some sort of mental closure. "Do you think it's over?"

"This crime spree?" Logan answered. "Yes, it's over—for now."

"What about that crossbreed bear? Do you think more of those things will come?"

"Nanulaks? Yes, I'm afraid they will."

"Why do you say that?"

"Pollution. Man disrespecting the earth, climate change…Take your pick."

"That's pretty fatalistic. Are there any other choices?"

"I can't think of any. The Ancient Ones would say that man has upset the climate wheel, changed the balance of life. Animals will fight to survive—it's in their nature."

"You're probably right, but that can't be good for us."

"No, it's not good for us, but at least now we know what's coming, I'll be...I mean, we'll be better prepared."

"For an invasion of mutant carnivores? How?"

"I don't know yet," Logan continued walking along the narrow ledge, "but it will come to me."

"OK...That's kind of a grim outlook. But on a positive note, we got the girl back safely," Billie Sue smiled as she motioned for Caroline to emerge from hiding in the darkness at the mouth of the cave. "That's really what this was all about."

"Small victories, Sheriff; you take them when you can."

"And I—I mean we—we solved the biggest crime spree in recent Deadraven history. That should get the town council off my back for now."

"All's well that ends well."

"I guess so," Sheriff Martin reflected. "You know, I owe you one," she glanced over at Raven, "both of you."

"For what?"

"For finding the girl, and for killing that...that Nanulak thing."

Raven and Logan exchanged a look.

"We were happy to help, Sheriff."

"Yeah. But when I think about it, how all this went down..."

"It was a long, strange trip," Logan agreed nonchalantly, looking down at the jagged cliffs below the trail.

"That's just it," Sheriff Martin scratched her head,

stopping for a moment, "I've got to write this one up in my report, but I'm not sure where to begin."

"How about we not write this one up? Why not just call it another one of our little secrets, Sheriff?"

"You're right, it may be best to keep this one to ourselves," Billie Sue laughed. "Wouldn't want the town folk to get all worked up about getting eaten alive by a Nanulak—bad for the tourist trade and all."

"Wheels of commerce. That's what's important in this town."

"Yeah, the wheels of commerce," Sheriff Martin paused. "All that aside, I've been thinking about what has happened over the last three weeks, and I just have one question for you."

"What's that, Sheriff?"

"Do you have some kind of…magical powers?" Billie Sue asked, dead serious.

"What?" Logan stopped along the trail. "What makes you ask that?"

"I'm asking because I saw a lot of bear tracks back there in that cave."

"Yeah, he must have been up here for quite a while."

"Probably so, but it's what I *didn't* see that bothers me."

"What would that be, Sheriff?"

"*Your* tracks."

"What do you mean?" Logan continued walking.

"I mean, after the lights went out, all hell broke loose. When the dust settled, you were gone and Sharon was talking crazy, right before she…"

"Bought the farm?"

"Yeah…all over me." Billie Sue looked down at her blood-splattered shirt. "That's the thing. When I made my way back out to the cave entrance, I didn't see any of your tracks leading out of the cave to the entrance...out on the ledge, where I found you and Raven at that fire ring with the...*bear*beque."

"No tracks of mine? Really?"

"Really."

Logan paused and then started walking again along the trail. "It was dark, Sheriff, confusing, and chaotic. Are you sure about the tracks in the cave? It was rather smoky in there."

"I'm pretty good at seeing things, and I'm really sure about what I didn't see."

"Really? Maybe that's where you and I are different...I'm not really sure about what I didn't see."

"All right, forget about the tracks that I didn't see. There's several more things don't add up."

"I'm listening, Sheriff, but we need to keep moving while we analyze your apprehensions."

Raven reassumed the lead, continuing on the narrow trail along the rock face leading away from the cave. Occasionally, a gust of wind forced them to pause and kneel down to avoid being swept over the cliff onto the sharp rocks, one thousand feet below.

"First off," Sheriff Martin continued, "the lights go out and you disappear. I hear the bear, but come to think of it, I never actually saw the bear. There's a struggle, a gunshot, and then I discover you and Raven outside with a big pile of *bear*beque."

"Like I said, Sheriff, it was pretty confusing back there. I heard the bear, just like you did. I figured we had a better chance of survival in the dark, so I tossed my jacket on the fire and tried to draw the animal away from you and Raven. It must have worked, because the Nanulak chased me away from all of you."

"Yeah, go on…"

"Somewhere in the cave," Logan explained, "I must have fallen, because I remember crawling at one point. I'm not sure how I ended up outside on the ledge. It was really smoky, though."

"But I keep thinking about it, and it doesn't make any sense. How did you get past me and the girl?"

"Maybe you shouldn't do that."

"Shouldn't do what?"

"Think about it. Sometimes, our mind can plays tricks on us, Sheriff. I don't really have an explanation, and besides, I thought you said this was going to be another one of our little secrets?"

"I know, I should let it go. But I need to know, you know?"

"Look, Sheriff, I'm not totally sure what happened in there myself. To be honest, I'm still trying to figure it out. There are a lot of things that I don't understand in this world, even now."

"OK, none of this makes any sense," Sheriff Martin laughed, and then turned serious. "Unless you're one of those…What do the Natives call them?"

"Skin walkers?"

Sheriff Martin locked her eyes on Logan, trying to read his reaction.

Raven shot a glance to Logan, which he deflected.

"You're not, are you?" Billie Sue repeated, sensing she'd hit a nerve.

"Not what?"

"One of those skin walker people."

Logan stopped walking and faced Billie Sue. He could see that now she was dead serious, and he wanted to provide her with something, anything that would help her mind make sense of the things she'd witnessed in the cave.

"Of course I'm not, Sheriff," Logan said in earnest. "From what I've heard, skin walkers are like the bogeyman your older brothers told you were in your closet. They're what was waiting for you to close your eyes, just so they could jump out and scare you. Skin walkers are just native legends, tall tales, stories told late at night around the campfire. They aren't real, Sheriff, any more than the bogeyman was in your childhood closet."

Billie Sue thought about it, and she did remember being terrified by her brothers as a child.

"My brothers, they would tell me that story, about the thing in my closet waiting for me to go to sleep…It scared the living crap out of me! They told me that the mound of dirt in the garden was a dead man's grave, and that if I picked the flowers on it, he'd come after me at night. Then they told me if I didn't believe them, the bogeyman would follow us to Grandma's house and hide in her basement, waiting for me to come down to the freezer to get ice cream."

"What happened then?"

"Well, after that, I never got any ice cream, and I never slept a wink at Grandma's house."

"That kind of thing happened to me too," Raven cut in, coming to Logan's defense. "Older brothers can be so mean."

"Besides," Logan continued, "if I was one those skin walker things, I'd know it, wouldn't I?"

"I guess you would," Sheriff Martin postulated. "But I don't really know how all that black magic works."

"You said two things bothered you," Logan said, pivoting to face her. "What else?"

"Oh yeah, the other thing…the gunshot."

"Gunshot?"

"Yes, just after the fire went out, there was a struggle, and a shot rang out. Sharon told me that the bear attacked her. Well, something sure as heck ripped out part of her throat, but she managed to get a shot off and wound it with her forty-five. She said she hit it point-blank in the left shoulder, but it didn't even slow it down."

"And?"

"I checked her gun when she was waking up; one shot was fired."

"Interesting…"

"What's interesting is that she says she shot the bear in the left shoulder, and you've got a gunshot wound on your left arm."

"This?" Logan rubbed his shoulder. "I didn't even notice it until we were outside on the ledge. It's just a scratch."

"Let me take a look at it," Sheriff Martin said as she examined the wound. "No, that's not a scratch, it's a gunshot wound all right, and it's a bad one."

"Maybe I got a through-and-through when Sharon shot the bear."

"Were you behind her?" the sheriff asked, trying to image the crime scene and bullet's trajectory.

"It was dark; I'm not sure where I was standing."

"A through-and-through; I guess that's possible…" Billie Sue stated skeptically.

"Or it could have been a ricochet. There're a lot of rocks in that cave; nowhere for a bullet to go except to rattle around for a while."

"Hmm…"

"I'm surprised you weren't hit too, Sheriff.

Anyway, it's nothing."

"Nothing?" Billie Sue said as she wrapped a torn piece of Logan's jacket around the wound. "A gunshot isn't nothing, but there, you'll live."

"Thanks," Logan rubbed his arm, appreciating the concern.

"But now I have another problem," Sheriff Martin exhaled. "Strict rules, you know. I have to make an official report whenever there's a gunshot injury." Billie Sue opened her logbook. "Damn paperwork never sleeps. It's just that..."

Logan could see she was struggling. "You're still bothered by something?"

"No, I'm good. It's just that my detective brain still doesn't know how to process this last part—the gunshot. I really have no logical explanation."

"Me neither, Sheriff."

Billie Sue closed the logbook, took a deep breath, and shoved it back into her pack. She leaned against the rocky ledge, thinking back before the most recent crime spree had begun.

"You know, I first heard about you from Search and Rescue. Got a call that some kid just appeared on the mountain and found a dead body before the scent dogs could even get out of the truck."

"Yeah, I saw them thrashing about. I could tell the dogs didn't really want to track that one. It looked like they needed some help."

"Some help? I know the lead investigator over there; he's been tracking up here for thirty years. Said he'd felt some disturbing sensations from time to time up on this mountain, but running into you? You totally spooked him."

"Spooked him, Sheriff? How?"

"Finding a body before the dogs, that's one thing, it happens, but he said when they caught up to you, you were just sitting there beside the body, talking to it, like it was still alive. You were asking questions, laughing, carrying on a conversation…that totally freaked him out. That's when he called me and suggested that maybe you'd be a better fit working murders and suicides with me."

"Do I spook you, Sheriff?"

"Honestly? Sometimes, you do."

"Why is that?"

"OK, confession time. When I used to work homicide in the big city…"

"You went from metro detective to boondocks po po? How did that happen?"

"Another story, another life—not important now. What it taught me was that when you investigate a death, in a way, you're speaking *for* the dead. But it seems like when you investigate a death, you're speaking *to* the dead…That's just got spooky crawling all over it."

Logan didn't respond, leaving an awkward pause.

"Things aren't always what they seem, Logan, especially here in Deadraven. Some people come here to find something, some to lose something. But we're all here for a reason; it just may not be obvious at first. It's like looking at a dead body; you have to look beyond what you see."

"Very perceptive, Sheriff."

"I know…I'm not as dumb as I look. I keep telling people that."

"That's not what I meant, no offense."

"None taken. Besides, sometimes it's safer to blend in than to stand out."

"I hear you."

"Look, forget town politics, that's for me to worry about. All that matters to me is that you help me close cases, and I appreciate that." Sheriff Martin paused, turning serious again.

"And whatever happened with you back there, I'm not complaining about it. I don't understand it, but I'm pretty sure we're all alive because of it. Here's the thing I do understand. Something else was with us in that cave; something downright evil…and I've got a strong feeling it meant to kill us all. But instead of running away from it, whatever it was, you turned out the lights and went after that thing by yourself. What the hell were you thinking?"

"Honestly, Sheriff? I wasn't thinking about it."

"OK. If you weren't thinking about it, what did you whisper to Raven just before you plunged us all into darkness?"

Logan paused for a moment; that was actually a question he could answer. "There's an old Indian saying, Sheriff: 'Any day is a good day to die.'"

"I've heard that before. What does that mean?"

"It means that if you're afraid to die, you can never live."

"Why do you say that?"

"Death is nothing to fear, Sheriff, it's just a change of worlds."

Billie Sue paused and looked into Raven's eyes, and then to Logan, suddenly realizing that she'd totally missed the complexity of the Native American spiritual connection between them.

"Oh…I get it now," Billie Sue deduced. "You two have been hanging out with that crazy Indian on Wuutaqa Mountain, haven't you? Ten Bears, that's his name, right?"

Logan exchanged a glance with Raven and smiled. "You've been checking up on us, Sheriff?"

"Yeah, part of my job. I am a detective, you know."

"OK, that's true. Since I returned to town, I've been seeking the counsel of Ten Bears. He's helping me...reconnect with my past."

"I thought he disowned you a while back. When you got shipped off to that reprogramming school. That's what I heard, anyway."

"Yes, there was a time when he, as you say, disowned me. Now, he and I have reached an... understanding."

"So would that make you the sorcerer's new apprentice?"

Logan was caught off guard by Sheriff Martin's directness and potential understanding of Native American culture.

"Sorcerer's apprentice? That would be an interesting job description, if such a thing existed," he countered. "But it's not really an accurate representation of our relationship."

"OK, then what would you call your...relationship?"

"Ten Bears is more like a mentor to me, a spiritual guide. He says that we all have a destiny to figure out, and he's helping me with mine."

"So what's your destiny?"

"I wish I knew, Sheriff. I'm still trying to figure that one out."

"Tell me about it," Billie Sue laughed.

"Now I'm the one who's curious, Sheriff. How did you know about that? The apprentice thing, with Ten

Bears, I mean."

"You're not the first cowboy at that rodeo." Billie Sue smiled.

"You? Really?"

"Yeah, well, I've heard stories. I'm part Shawnee. You didn't know that, did you?"

"What happened?"

"Got bucked off that horse a long time ago…but that's another story, another time."

Chapter 48: Ascension

Raven led the party down the narrow trail along the edge of the rock face, where she stopped, peeled back some bushes, and revealed a vertical crack in the boulders. Inside the fissure was a rickety old wooden ladder that led deeper into the rocky opening until it disappeared into the shadows of the crevice.

"We're not going back down in that cave, are we?" Sheriff Martin asked hesitantly.

"No, we're not going down," Raven answered, as she dropped her backpack and steadied the ladder. "We're going up...through the keyhole to the sky."

Ten minutes after entering the shadows and carefully climbing the wobbly ladder into the fissure, they finally could see a beam of light above them. The hole in the rocks above was small and forced them to shed their backpacks to fit in between the boulders one at a time as they scaled the last section of ladders out of the shadows. After several switchbacks and a couple of broken ladder rungs, they emerged into the sunlight on top of a large, flat rock overlooking an Alpine mesa.

"Welcome to Sky Kiva," Raven announced. "We should be able to get a signal out up here."

"A signal?" Sheriff Martin questioned.

"A satellite upload from the tracker beacon," Logan answered. "Hit the emergency button, and it should get picked up by the IERCC in Houston. They'll relay our position to local Search and Rescue."

"Really?"

"Yes, the weather's cleared enough for them to get a bird up now if we hurry."

"Just hit the button? That's all it takes to get us out of here?"

"No, there's one more thing. Somebody's going to have to pick up the tab for an emergency chopper ride. Search and Rescue will be sending somebody a ginormous bill."

"My dad will pay," Caroline spoke up. "The beacon's on his account anyway."

"Works for me," Sheriff Martin agreed as she pressed the orange button on the tracker beacon. "My account would say, 'declined due to insufficient everything.'"

While Raven and Logan sat down and scanned the horizon for the helicopter, Billie Sue pulled out her logbook for one last entry. After several attempted descriptions and rewrites of the crime spree, she tore out the page, crumpled it up, and tossed it over the cliff.

"Trouble with your paperwork, Sheriff?" Logan asked.

"Yeah, writer's block again."

"How far did you get?"

"OK, here we go. The lost girl is safe. We tracked her kidnapper, an escaped mental patient who was impersonating her dead sister, a park ranger that she allegedly killed, to a hidden cave that's not on any map, where she was attacked by a mutant bear that I never actually saw, just before she killed herself."

"Hmmm."

"I'm going with 'the lost girl is safe' for now; details to follow."

"Sometimes less is more, Sheriff."

"Word," Billie Sue smiled.

After an hour or so, a faint thumping sound could

be heard lumbering its way through the canyons from below. Logan stood and waved his jacket as the Search and Rescue helicopter finally emerged from the clouds and hovered above the Alpine mesa. One by one, the rescue crew lowered the metal cage from the belly of the chopper as the weary companions strapped on the harness and were plucked from the rocky mountaintop. Safely inside, the pilot nodded to Logan, and the helicopter lurched upward, leaving the mountains of the snowcapped Continental Divide shrouded in the clouds of the setting sun.

"Hey," Sheriff Martin tugged on Logan's jacket, pointing out the window, "who's that down there?"

Logan wiped the fog from the bay door window and could just make out an old man, dressed in elkskins and holding a charred wooden staff, perched on the edge of the tree line beneath a small cabin wedged in the rocks. It was Ten Bears, his eyes locked on the metal bird as it descended into the canyon to avoid the high winds above.

"Can you drop us over there?" Logan shouted as he tapped the pilot on the shoulder. "At the cliff face near that cabin."

"Why?" Sheriff Martin shouted above the low drone of the machine.

"Now I have to file my report," Logan laughed. "Duties of an apprentice, remember?"

"Oh sure, go debrief the sorcerer. Just catch me up on at least some of the real story sometime, won't you?"

"Will do," Logan shouted back as the helicopter hovered over the cliff, swirling snow in all directions.

"Wait!" Sheriff Martin yelled just before Logan disembarked, handing him the signal beacon. "You might need this."

"What for?" Logan shouted as he stepped into the doorway.

"In case you get lost again. But the next ride's on your tab."

Logan smiled and leaned back in to whisper in the sheriff's ear, "You get Caroline to the hospital."

"I will," Sheriff Martin smiled.

"And contact her parents on the way; they'll be worried," Raven shouted.

"That's one call I'm glad to make," Billie Sue acknowledged, rubbing her forehead. "And then there's the other call for recovering a body on sacred tribal lands that's not on any map, where I had no jurisdiction or authorization to be, in a place that can never be revealed. A little help, here?"

"I'll see what I can do, Sheriff. Catch you on the other side," Logan barked as he hopped out of the bay door and landed in a snowbank. He sprang to his feet and waved the pilot off.

"The other side?" Billie Sue yelled back as the chopper took off. "The other side of what?"

Chapter 49: Reunion

The Search and Rescue helicopter slowly ascended from the cliff face, hovered for a moment, and then pitched sideways into the wind. It headed down the mountain to the Deadraven Medical Center. Sheriff Martin held the exhausted kidnap victim's head in her lap; she'd fallen asleep to the rhythmic thumping of the chopper blades beating against the wind.

As the helicopter cleared the tree line down the mountain, a blast of cold air swept over the rock face near the cabin, bringing snow flurries back to the Continental Divide; another storm was blowing in.

"I am glad to see you alive in this world," Ten Bears exclaimed in an unusual burst of emotion as he hugged Raven and Logan.

"Me too," Raven smiled.

Ten Bears noticed the wound and bandage on Logan's arm, reaching out to touch it gently.

"We have much to talk about, Niwot. I want to know everything that happened. But let us talk inside, out of the storm," he said, motioning toward Radio's cabin just ahead.

Logan nodded, and they quickly made their way along the icy trail in blowing snow until they arrived at the cabin door. Before they could knock, the door swung open and an eager, wide-eyed Radio rolled onto the porch to greet them.

"Truth Detector? Thank God you're both safe! And the kidnapped girl? Did you find her in time?"

"She's alive, safe and sound." Logan put his hand on Radio's shoulder. "Thanks to you, my friend."

"Holy freaking crap, I was scared," Radio exhaled, now noticing that Logan and Raven were not alone. "Oh, excuse me. Introductions? I'm…Wait, let's get you out of this weather first. What am I thinking? I don't get many guests up here. Come in!"

Radio and Ten Bears greeted each other, exchanged introductions, and then they settled down in front of the roaring fire to warm their tired bodies.

"What happened up there?" Radio asked.

"Yes, Niwot," Ten Bears echoed. "Tell me of your vision quest."

"It's a long story," Logan began. "The official report is: 'The lost girl is safe.' That's all that matters."

Ten Bears studied Logan's face, sensing that he was hesitant to go into too many details of his vision quest in mixed company.

"Tell me the short version at least," Radio begged.

"OK, we tracked the mental patient and the kidnapped girl to a cave just below Sky Kiva," Logan continued. "She abducted her at Wapiti Meadows and held her at gunpoint in the cave, but she never harmed the girl."

"What happened in the cave?"

"That's the long version of the story. The short story is, the girl is safe and her kidnapper took her own life."

"Man!" Radio groaned. "Suicide? Why does it always end that way up here?"

"Yes, it is a sad tale," Ten Bears commented. "This mountain has claimed many troubled souls."

"Hey, what about the ranger?" Radio asked. "The one over at the park service?"

"The real ranger? She didn't make it either," Logan added.

"But how…"

"Shot dead, but that's another long story."

"Well hell's bells!" Radio exclaimed as he looked outside at the gathering storm; it was snowing sideways again. "Two more dead bodies. I may as well put on the kettle; nobody's going anywhere tonight. And I want to hear the whole story, Truth Detector—the complete, unedited, long-play version this time."

"As do I," Ten Bears chimed in. "But a cup of hot tea first sounds good. Let me give you a hand."

As Radio rolled across the floor to his rack of dried plants and shelves of mason jars, Ten Bears studied the flowers in one particular container.

"I see you have quite a wildflower collection." Ten Bears opened a jar and smelled the contents.

"Yeah, I like to gather these alpine plants. They only grow during summer in one place up here on the mountain, you know."

"Ah, summer," Ten Bears laughed. "That would be the two weeks just after winter?"

"And the two weeks before the next winter."

"What is your special brew for tonight, my friend?"

"Well, I like to experiment with different blends of my flowers for tea," Radio continued.

"Yes, I see," Ten Bears commented. "Many of the wildflowers that grow above the timberline have certain, shall we say, unique properties."

"Yeah, man! I've discovered that. Even better than the medicinal herbs I was getting over in the Middle East. I like to try different combinations, you know, just to see what kind of bang I can get."

Radio paused and then selected two jars of dried flowers from the shelf, one of which Ten Bears had smelled earlier.

"This should make an interesting blend," he said, placing the jars on the counter beside the boiling kettle. "I haven't tried them together yet, but these little buds are two of my favorite purple flowers. I like purple."

As Radio picked up the kettle, Ten Bears gently put his hand over his cup to prevent Radio from pouring.

"Excuse me," Ten Bears cautioned, "but if you blend those two plants together, you will get that bang you are looking for."

"Really? Why?"

"One of those is mountain nightshade; you will be dead in sixty seconds, my friend."

"Whoa, that would be harsh!" Radio opened his eyes in embarrassment. "I didn't know, man. I saw a rabbit eating them, so I assumed it was OK. I've just been experimenting with these plants and flowers, you know, sort of trial and error."

"I'm afraid that blend would be one trial and all error," Ten Bears counseled, noticing Radio's long face. "Not to worry, there is no book on these rare flowers to follow, so do not feel bad."

"I'm glad you're here," Radio blushed. "Or there'd be one more dead body on the mountain tonight."

"You are welcome, my friend. You have watched over Niwot on his vision quest, and for that, I am grateful. Let me have my granddaughter teach you the ancient art of high country tea making."

"I'd appreciate learning about tea making, mostly the trial without the error part."

"And the art of not poisoning yourself?"

"That part, especially."

Raven had been listening and came over to the kitchen to examine the dried flowers, raised her eyebrow, and made an alternate selection.

"Let's start with these," she said, carefully selecting two different flowers and then pouring a cup for Radio.

He let the aroma of the brew drift up his face and into his nostrils before closing his eyes and taking a sip.

"Mmm…that smells…heavenly," Radio sighed.

"And not at all poisonous," Raven added.

"What else could a man ask for?"

Chapter 50: The Truth

With a good cup of steamy hot tea in his hands, Radio rolled over to the fireplace where Logan and Raven were warming their bodies. Ten Bears was enjoying his own cup of tea, gazing out the window at the raging snowstorm descending on the mountain.

"Now that we're settled in for the night, Truth Detector," Radio said, "tell me, what's really going on up here?"

"What do you mean?"

"You know what I'm talking about," Radio insisted. "What I hear on my scanners: all the suicides, murders, and now these kidnappings on the mountain."

"Yes, I know what you're talking about."

"Look, I've been in two wars. Lots more if you count smoking some terrorists with a drone while they're sleeping in their tents. I've seen some bad shit, man, but I'm used to that. My shrink at the VA says I've become desensitized to death—maybe he's right. But this voice that tells me, in advance, that someone's going to die? Why is she telling me? That voice has me, well, freaked out, man."

Ten Bears exchanged a look with Logan, put his hand on his shoulder and then walked over to poke the fire. After a moment of staring at the flames, he turned to Radio and spoke softly.

"There are strange things that happen on this mountain, my friend, this is true. I will tell you a story, but you must hold it close, for this is a story that I do not tell often. It is also a story that I do not tell to those outside our clan, but for you, I will make an exception.

I will tell this story because it seems that each of our lives in this room have become intertwined. As a spider weaves its web, drawing in all those around her, you have now become attached to our web. You have become part of the story, and because of that, you deserve to know the truth."

Ten Bears looked at Logan and smiled before turning back to Radio. "The truth, my friend," Ten Bears continued, "is a rare commodity these days, and especially on this mountain."

"I can handle the truth," Radio volunteered. "It's the lies that I don't handle so well. I can smell a lie from a mile away, you know. That's why I sought out my friend here, the Truth Detector, when that 'guy fell down in the woods' hogwash up at Spirit Lake came out."

"I believe you," Ten Bears said, studying Radio's face. "You are a man who deserves to understand, to know the truth." He carefully reached inside his coat and pulled out a worn buffalo-skin rattle filled with quartz crystals and shook it, producing random flashes of light that bounced off the ceiling and filled the cabin with an iridescent glow.

"The story that I am about to tell is a sacred story, and sacred stories can only be told and listened to during dark nights, in the dead of winter. Now the spirits are gathered with us to help me tell the story."

Radio's eyes were wide open as he stared into the glowing rattle Ten Bears held in his hand.

"But if I am to tell you this story, I cannot start from where we are; I must start from where it began."

"Now that sounds like the long version coming, mind if I get my pipe?" Radio asked. "It's been a while since I've heard a good story up here."

"By all means," Ten Bears paused, reaching into his medicine pouch. "I think it is time we all had a smoke."

Chapter 51: Ancient Secrets

As Radio puffed away on the pipe of special tobacco Ten Bears had offered for his story, smoke rings of truth began to fill the cabin with understanding. Radio's eyes grew wide as Ten Bears recounted the origin of the strange tales of what would one day come to be the hidden secrets of Deadraven, nestled high in the Rocky Mountains.

"Our people have known since the beginning," Ten Bear began, "that this mountain was a sacred place—a dangerous place, a spiritual place that must be respected. This is why no Indian tribes would live here on Thunderbird Mountain, even though the high valley below is blessed with clear streams and abundant wildlife. This mountain is, as my Hopi brothers call it, '*Koyonakasti*,' a world out of balance."

"I heard that," Radio interrupted, puffing on his pipe.

"Generations ago," Ten Bears continued, "when the first trappers came, we told them to stay away, but they would not listen. Then the trappers guided white settlers here. Most of them either died mysteriously or left quickly, never to return. Those that managed to survive would never say why they left, only later secretly agreeing with us that no man should live on this mountain."

"Then how did a town spring up?" Radio asked, leaning forward in his wheelchair.

"One day, a settler named Jedidiah Livingstone came to the *'never summer mountain'* to stake his claim. He climbed the highest peak along the Continental Divide, and after taking a fall over a rocky cliff that should have claimed his life, he stumbled into the very cave that Logan and Raven discovered. It was there, when he crossed the old rope bridge over the River of Lost Souls, that he encountered a giant bear inside, guarding the cave. His foolishness had awakened the bear from deep within the mountain, and the bear was angry. The bear played with him like a cat plays with a mouse before it devours its prey, until finally it grew bored and was ready to kill him. The white man was terrified and begged for his life. Strangely enough, the bear hesitated for a moment, listening to his plea.

"'Spare me,' the white man pleaded, 'and I will be forever in your debt.'

"The giant bear laughed as it prepared to kill him, but then, always enjoying a game of wits, the bear stopped to answer the feeble proposal. 'What would you offer me to spare your life?'

"The white man was confused, and in his haste, he made a proposition: 'Grant me my life and I will give you…the lives of many others.'

"'Go on,' the bear answered, now intrigued.

"'Let me live here and prosper,' the white man bargained, 'and in exchange, you can take some of the others that come. I will bring them to you.'

"'Why should I trust you?' the bear countered in suspicion. 'If you bring more people to this mountain, then surely they will try to kill me.'

"'No, they will not,' the white man argued. 'I will protect you.'

"'You? How will you protect me?'

"'I will protect you with whatever it takes,' the white man pronounced, regaining his confidence. He stood up, aimed his rifle, and shot a raven from a perch high above them. The bird fell between the bear and the man; it was dead.

"'There is power in your words and your fire stick,' the bear observed. 'You are clever indeed, not unlike me. I have decided. I will spare your life today, and in exchange, you will protect me from your kind, with, as you say, *whatever it takes*. And you will guide lost souls to me to be taken at my will. That is our bargain.'

"'Yes,' the white man agreed. 'I live, I will protect you, and I will guide lost souls to you…just don't take too many.'

"The bear raked his claws across the man's chest, knocking him unconscious. 'The scar on your chest shall be the sign of our Covenant,' the bear laughed. 'Now go and do my bidding.'"

"So that is how the Covenant of the Mountain came to pass?" Logan interrupted.

"Yes," Ten Bears sighed as he puffed on the pipe. "As it was, as it is, and in this world, as it ever shall be. And that is how the first white man survived here in the shadow of the mountain; with the Covenant, and the birth of the town that the white men now call Deadraven."

"That's a heavy trip," Radio whistled. "What happened after that?"

"What happened?" Ten Bears continued. "A birthright of murder and suicide was born. Many in this valley are direct descendants of Jedidiah Livingstone, and many of them have sworn to carry on his legacy today. Those that do so, secretly carry the sign of the bear."

Radio reflected on the gravity of Ten Bears' words.

"I'm still confused. I think I understand about the bear, but why did Guardian call out to me through the ether?"

"What you heard on the wind was the sound of good and evil in conflict. The shadow of the mountain calls, and the unfortunate heed his call. Sometimes, souls that are taken willingly, the souls that contemplate taking their own lives, change their minds and call out for help. Guardian is a spirit who listens for those calls and tries to help them. For reasons known only to her, she chose you as her helper. Maybe this is because she heard your voice in the ether and she thought you were a Wind Talker as well."

"A Wind Talker?" Radio echoed as a burst of static came across his scanner. "Spirits talking to me? Now you're really freaking me out."

Chapter 52: Purpose

As his past life of war memories flashed through his mind, Radio sat there in silence.

"A Wind Talker," he repeated softly. "The radio man, that's all I was. But in the heat of battle, my voice would often be the difference between life and death for our soldiers—for my friends."

"In your own way, you are a Wind Talker," Ten Bears acknowledged.

"I guess I am," Radio admitted. "It's kind of creepy, but now that you describe it, it's like déjà vu or something. I've been down that road in combat, where around every corner, lurking in the shadows, there was someone or something waiting to kill you. It could have been anyone, a face in the crowd, a woman carrying groceries, a sniper on a roof, an IED…You let your guard down, you trust anyone, and you're dead."

"To be the eyes and ears of warriors engaged in battle? You stood guard over the lives of others; this was a noble cause, my friend," Ten Bears offered support. "But at times, I am sure it was a heavy load to bear."

"Yeah, I've been there," Radio confessed. "When we were in country, the voice of death was all around us. I could hear it whispering to me in my sleep, calling out, taunting me."

There was an eerie silence that hung in the room as Radio processed the strange similarities of his war-torn past and the life that had somehow led him to this mountain. *It was the same life*, he thought, *just a different enemy, a different battlefield.*

"Sir!" Radio snapped to attention, facing Ten Bears. "I understand the mission, and I'm ready for duty. I'll need to recalibrate my equipment, but may I ask one question, sir?"

"You may," Ten Bears answered.

"Am I correct in understanding that this shadow enemy you describe has hostile guerilla forces blended into the local landscape?"

"That is true."

"Then how can it be defeated, sir? I mean, I assume we aren't going with a scorched-earth policy."

"That is the question, indeed, my friend. How can we defeat our enemy?" Ten Bears studied the man in the wheelchair, the rigidness of his posture and the steely focus of his eyes.

"I can see that you are prepared for battle, soldier, but here is our dilemma. The evil that lives on this mountain has great power, like a spider with many dangerous webs to spin. It is an evil that will be difficult to defeat. We may never be able to exterminate it, but I believe we can hold it in check. The battle ahead is as you have envisioned with one exception; it is we that are the guerilla force. Together, we are destined to be a thorn in the side of evil. I believe this is why we are here, all of us, including you, my friend. It is our destiny."

Radio looked around the room at Logan, Raven, and Ten Bears.

"Four of us against a powerful, unknown enemy with a secret guerilla force embedded with the locals?"

"That is the mission, soldier."

Radio thought about the call of duty as outlined by Ten Bears. After contemplating the operation, he spun back around in his wheelchair. "Permission to speak freely, sir?"

"By all means, my friend."

"An old man, two kids, and a disabled veteran with, well, anger management issues. As a fighting force, sir, we are…insignificant."

Ten Bears stood and warmed his hands by the fire. "Let me tell you another story, soldier. A grain of sand seems insignificant compared to an oyster, would you agree?"

"Yes…"

"But from that insignificant grain of sand, the overwhelming power of the oyster can be thwarted, and a positive outcome can occur."

"I don't understand, sir."

"The oyster swallows a grain of sand. The grain of sand irritates the oyster, and they struggle for, what we shall call their collective destiny. No matter how much they struggle, the oyster and the sand remain unchanged. They hold each other in check, as neither will yield to the other. But because of their struggle, a beautiful pearl is created. And in the end, the struggle becomes the pearl that defines their destiny."

Radio cocked his head, trying to understand Ten Bears' parable of the oyster. "I've been told all my life that I'm an irritant," Radio laughed. "Now you're telling me that I'm a grain of sand, I'm an irritant, and it's a good thing?"

"For those that choose the path, it is the only thing," Ten Bears added.

"Then I'm an irritant," Radio pronounced. "Hell, we're all irritants!"

"The Irritants? Sounds like a punk rock band," Logan injected. "We get under your skin!"

"Hell yeah!" Radio exclaimed, throwing his head

back and feigning an air guitar solo.

"I like you, my friend," Ten Bears laughed. "I sense that you and I have many more stories to share. We should continue our stories at my lodge."

"Why?" Radio came down from his rock band high.

"There is a saying that goes, 'He who tells the stories, controls the world.' We will smoke a pipe, take a sweat together, and tell more stories. Then we will see what comes."

"Truth be told, my pipe's getting kinda empty here," Radio said, tapping his can of medicinal leaves. "Can't get down the hill to the store very often, so coming to your lodge? That could be a good thing."

"Excellent," Ten Bears exclaimed. "And Raven will make us her special tea; it will be both refreshing and non-lethal."

The smile faded from Radio's face as his mind drifted back to his days of war and the memory of fallen comrades that he left behind. Those friendships, forged in the heat of battle, they were bonds that would last lifetimes, lifetimes that were now gone. Since he'd been discharged, Radio had never felt a connection to any other human being. Most civilians couldn't understand what he'd been through—the horror, the chaos, the cold sweats in the night, the voice of death calling to him. They couldn't understand what it was like trying to protect your friends from an unknown enemy determined to kill all of you at any moment. They couldn't understand what it was like to put your life in the hands of someone else, every day and every night, knowing he would lay down his life to protect you as well. No, Radio had never felt a connection after the war to anyone else that understood him, until now.

"I can see the dark clouds in your eyes," Ten Bears put his hand on Radio's shoulder. "It is the sadness of a warrior who has lost comrades in battle. It is a sadness that I know as well."

"That war…it's my own private hell," Radio wiped a tear from his eyes, "but being alone is its own type of war."

"It is indeed, my friend. But this I have also learned from war: it is that warriors should never fight alone. Come, smoke and drink with me. This is what warriors do when a great battle is over. You have earned it, my friend; we all have."

"You know, that's pretty much what we did over there after every skirmish," Radio laughed. "Mostly, the drinking part."

"Good, then you will come. It will cleanse your spirit and prepare you for our next battle."

"You should know," Radio confessed, wiping a tear from his eye, "I've done some bad things. War can change a man; it can make you do things to survive, things you want to forget. Now that you bring it up, I guess my spirit could use some cleansing."

Chapter 53: Slumber Party

As the clock on the cabin wall struck midnight, Radio yawned and shifted in his wheelchair. The hour was late, and with the adventures of the last few weeks, he was exhausted. "I hate to break up the party, but I figure we all need some sleep, although for me, it'll probably be another fitful night. Help yourself to the sleeping bags over there by the fire."

"Where do you sleep best?" Raven asked.

"Most nights, right here in this chair." Radio yawned as he rolled across the floor and shut down his command center. "Too much damn trouble to get in and out of the bed, anyway."

Logan followed Radio across the room and put his arm around his shoulder. "Without your help," Logan whispered, "things wouldn't have ended as they did today."

"Ironic, isn't it? You know, I was giving serious thought to cashing in my chips before I met you, Truth Detector. If I had, I'd been just another one of those lost souls, a lonely voice floating on the ether."

"I know how you feel," Logan acknowledged. "With the hand that life's dealt me, I confess I've checked my own cards a few times."

"Seriously, I tried for years to get someone to listen to me, anyone, but it was like no one could hear me. That is, until you came along. You listened, and you heard me. You were the only one that would really talk with me."

"Not true. Guardian chose to talk with you."

"Yeah, you're right. But I still can't figure that one

out."

"It was because she believed in you."

"But why?"

"I don't know," Logan wondered, "but Guardian trusts that you have a purpose in this world. People come up to this mountain to experience the natural beauty of the wilderness, but standing in the middle of it, most of them can't see the forest for the trees. You can see both, my friend; that is a rare quality indeed."

"Want to know a secret?" Radio leaned over to Logan. "I'm just glad to finally have a job to do again— any job. That feels good, man. But you know what else would feel good? To get a decent night's sleep; I've haven't slept in what seems like forever."

"Stand down, soldier, your job is done for now," Logan comforted Radio as he closed his eyes. "You will sleep well tonight."

"Will I dream, Truth Detector? Dreams of truth?"

"You will."

"How do you know?" Radio mumbled as he started to drift off.

"Because the Ancient Ones say that, 'Dreams are the only truth, until we awake.'"

As Radio fell quickly into a deep sleep, Logan walked back across the room and sat down beside Ten Bears.

"You are learning, Niwot," Ten Bears said softly as he placed his hand on Logan's shoulder.

Raven observed her grandfather's exchange of praise for Logan and smiled; the boy he had once banished was the man he now had forgiven.

Ten Bears picked up one of the sleeping bags, wrapped it around his body, and curled up next to the fire. "In the old days," Ten Bears joked, "we all slept under a buffalo hide in the nude. That was a time of happy dreams."

"These aren't the old days anymore, Grandfather," Raven corrected him.

"Well, I am sleeping in the nude."

"We didn't need to know that."

"I always have, I always will. It is tradition."

"OK, we'll take the other sleeping bag. Good night."

"But no sleeping in the nude for you two," Ten Bears teased.

"Yes, Grandfather," Raven mumbled, now embarrassed.

As Logan and Raven snuggled into their sleeping bag, Ten Bears began snoring like a lumberjack.

"I'm glad you came back," Raven whispered.

"Me too," Logan exhaled as Raven slid her body close to his inside the sleeping bag.

"This is our first night sleeping together," Raven spoke softly into Logan's ear.

Ten Bears rolled over and snorted next to them before settling back to sleep.

"It's not quite as I imagined it would be," Raven giggled.

"Me neither," Logan exhaled.

"So…You have thought about it?"

"Thought about what?"

"Us…sleeping together."

"Of course," Logan admitted; now it was his turn to be embarrassed.

Ten Bears tossed about and continued snoring.

"It's just that when I thought about us sleeping together, it didn't include your grandfather lying next to us in the nude, making those…well…noises."

Raven laughed aloud, trying to cover her mouth so as to not wake her grandfather. She sighed and wrapped her legs around Logan, rubbing her hips gently next to his.

"Next time," Raven whispered, "it will be more."

Chapter 54: Daybreak

As morning broke across the Continental Divide, the storm finally had cleared after dropping several feet of new snow above the tree line. Ten Bears sat on the front porch, his eyes closed, soaking in the warmth of the sunrise as it slipped over the jagged peaks of the Rocky Mountains.

Inside the cabin, Logan awoke to the muffled softness of Raven's body wrapped around his, her head nuzzled into the back of his neck.

"If this is a dream," Logan whispered, "I don't want to wake up."

The sudden sound across the room of Radio wheezing in his sleep startled Raven. She stretched and hugged Logan around the waist gently, slowly opening her eyes.

"Do you think we should wake him?" Raven yawned and snuggled back against Logan's warm body.

"No, let him sleep," Logan said softly as he wiggled out of her arms and the sleeping bag. "He deserves some peace for once."

On the porch, Ten Bears opened his eyes, steadied himself with his staff and stood, stretched, and then quietly opened the door to the cabin.

"Good morning, lovebirds," he teased.

Logan looked away, not sure how to handle the attention.

"In some tribes," Ten Bears goaded as he put his arm around Logan, "you two would be considered married now."

"Grandfather!" Raven hissed with embarrassment.

"Just for the record," Logan confessed, "nothing happened! I swear!"

"Do not worry," Ten Bears laughed, putting his arm around Logan. "The same thing happened to me once. But as I remember, I was much older."

"Enough!" Raven shoved herself in between Logan and her grandfather, scolding them both. "You are like little boys."

"She is right," Ten Bears admitted. "I was just having some fun with you two."

"What about Radio?" Raven injected, changing the subject. "Will he be OK if we leave him here?"

"As long as Guardian leaves him alone, he'll sleep for a week," Logan answered.

"And how about you, Niwot?" Ten Bears asked, now being serious. "Will you sleep as well?"

"Soon," Logan answered, looking out the window. "I will sleep, but first I need to make one more stop."

"I thought you might," Ten Bears smiled.

Before Raven could question what they were talking about, a thumping noise reverberated off the canyon walls and across the icy peaks of the mountain. Logan stepped out of the cabin, off the porch and waved his jacket over his head, signaling the approaching Apache helicopter. The chopper recognized his signal, dipped in between the rocks, and set down gently on a flat rock fifty yards from the cabin. Raven took one last look at Radio sleeping peacefully, closed the door, and joined Logan by the chopper. As they ducked their heads and boarded, Logan flashed a smile at the pilot.

"Got your reservation for the afternoon shuttle," Cody Winston shouted above the noise of the engine.

"So when did you get your pilot's license?" Logan

barked back.

"After Flyboy got his ride," Cody smiled, glancing over at her grinning copilot. "Man, that guy likes to ride."

"On the Knucklehead?"

"Oh, yeah, on that too," Cody winked. "Where to?"

"The Tea Haus," Logan yelled back as he slammed the bay door shut.

"Roger that," Cody acknowledged. "One latte to go."

Chapter 55: Illusions

Piloting the Apache helicopter, Cody Winston circled the trees surrounding the Timberline Tea Haus and then skillfully maneuvered the chopper to a perfect landing on a ledge above the upper parking lot.

"You're one smooth operator," her flyboy copilot complimented.

"You're not so bad yourself," Cody winked and leaned over for a kiss.

"Good," Logan interrupted as he hopped out the bay door. "The lights are still on; she's here. Keep the motor running, I'll just be a minute."

"Don't be too long," Cody shot back. "We've got to get this bird back to the nest before breakfast."

Out the side window of the helicopter, Raven and Ten Bears watched as Logan descended the rocky path and entered the front door of the deserted Tea Haus. On the roof, vandals had shot out the lights of the neon sign long ago. The windows along the deck that weren't covered in plywood were shattered as well.

"No one else has been in there in ten years," Cody sighed. "Kind of a spooky place, but for some reason, it's his favorite hangout."

"Really?" Raven questioned.

"Yeah, I've dropped him off here many a night, not to see him again until dawn, sacked out on the sofa in my garage."

"What does he do in there?"

"Beats the hell out of me," Cody said, puzzled. "We have this kind of 'don't ask, don't tell' thing going on. Someday, maybe he'll explain it to me…or then again, knowing Logan, maybe not."

"We've got to go," the copilot interrupted, tapping his watch.

"OK, right," Cody acknowledged. "Sorry, folks, but the ride's over for today. Tell Logan we had to fly."

Raven and Ten Bears hopped out of the chopper and closed the cargo bay door. They waved goodbye as Cody Winston carefully took off, cleared the trees, and pitched the helicopter into the canyon and back to base.

"The Apache is a nice bird," Ten Bears said and smiled at Raven. "But not as graceful as a Thunderbird...or a White Owl."

Chapter 56: The Bargain

Seated on a boulder above the run-down Tea Haus, Raven and Ten Bears sat in silence, watching sunlight stream down from the mountaintops into the valley. Above them in the cobalt blue sky, the screech of a hawk echoed off the canyon walls to the slumbering town below.

"Why are we here, Grandfather?" Raven finally asked.

"We are here," Ten Bears said, "because Niwot seeks closure with her."

"He's here to talk to a…girl?" Raven bristled.

"Yes," Ten Bears answered. "But it is not what you think."

"How do you know what I think?"

"I see the way you look at him, my Raven, and if that look is true, you will need to find a way to understand."

"Understand what?"

"That we are here because this is part of Niwot's life. It is a part that he must live with, a part that we must learn to accept."

"What is it, Grandfather?"

"It is something that I put in motion many years ago."

Ten Bears put his arm around Raven, hugging her. After a moment, he continued with his explanation. "When Logan confronted the Shadow Bear in the cave many years ago, you were there also."

"I know. He saved my life."

"Yes, he saved your life, and I in turn saved his."

"What?"

"It was his courage that allowed you to escape the Shadow Bear, but that was not his fate; Logan did not escape. The Shadow Bear caught him on the old rope bridge; it ripped open his chest with its massive claws and tossed him in the pool. That is when I confronted the Shadow Bear. The Shadow Bear knew who I was, and of my power, so we...negotiated."

"Negotiated?"

"Yes, we made a bargain."

"What kind of bargain?"

"In our world, a life can be taken, but a spirit must be surrendered—either voluntarily or in battle. The Shadow Bear knew that he could not take the spirit of a child; the Ancient Ones would never allow this."

"What did you offer him as a bargain?"

"I told the Shadow Bear that if he would release Logan's spirit from the pool, he would return to face him in battle when he was of age."

"Why would the Shadow Bear agree to your bargain?"

"Because I also told him that when Logan returned, he would not run away; he would face the Shadow Bear, without my help. If he defeated Logan, he could take his spirit, and mine as well."

"You said your bargain with the Shadow Bear was for Logan's spirit," Raven questioned. "Not Niwot. Why?"

"Truth in the wrong hands," Ten Bears advised, "can be deadly. If the Shadow Bear had known of Logan's heritage then, and what he could become, he would not be here today."

Raven thought back to the chaos of that day in the cave and shuddered. "And you never told either of us the truth, all these years?"

"What I told you of that day, it was the truth," Ten Bears reasoned. "Just not all of the truth. You are everything to me, my Raven—you know this. But you were too young then to know what you know now. Since that day in the cave long ago, you have had ten years of training and practice, ten years of knowledge and experience. Today, your heart can handle the truth, the whole truth."

Raven thought for a moment; some things that had been a mystery in her past were starting to come into focus. But even with the revelation that Ten Bears had just disclosed, there were still many unanswered questions. "Grandfather, when you made your bargain with the Shadow Bear, weren't you afraid that both of your spirits would be lost?"

"Yes, that was the risk I took. But without the bargain in the cave for Logan that day, Niwot's spirit would never be."

Ten Bears stared up at the puffy white clouds in the sky, forming shapes and then dissipating as they swirled into the heavens.

"My days will soon pass," he continued, "but Niwot had his whole life in front of him. While I knew very early in my heart that he was willing to trade his life for yours, what I did not know was who he would become...that was up to him. When the Shadow Bear took his life that day, I knew I had to do something. I chose to trust more in Niwot's spirit than in the power of the Shadow Bear. I knew he just needed time and space to find his way. That is why I sent him away, to grow stronger and discover his inner strength. But I did not send him on his journey alone; I made sure that he would find guidance along the way."

Ten Bears' words washed across Raven's mind in a stream of confusion and understanding.

"So everything that happened yesterday in the cave, that was all a part of your bargain?"

"Yes, it was. And with your help, that part of the bargain was fulfilled."

"That part?" Raven questioned. "There is more?"

"There is always more," Ten Bears smiled.

Chapter 57: Lessons Learned

Inside the Timberline Tea Haus, Logan slid into a booth and closed his weary eyes for a moment. It had been a restless night for him in the sleeping bag at Radio's cabin, and after the emotional whirlwind of the last three weeks, he was both physically and mentally exhausted.

"You look like you could use a hot cup of tea," the waitress said softly, touching Logan's shoulder. He winced, the adrenaline from the battle with the Shadow Bear in the cave was wearing off and the pain from the gunshot wound on his arm was throbbing.

"OK, that's starting to hurt now," Logan admitted.

"Are you all right?" the waitress asked as she examined the bandage. "I've got some pain pills in the kitchen—they're prescription. I used to use them for my back."

"No thanks, I'm all right," Logan lied, trying to suppress the ache. "It's just a scratch, really." He took a deep breath, focused on the beautiful brown eyes of the waitress, and somehow, his pain subsided.

"I heard some of the police chatter yesterday on my scanner; they were quite frantic. What happened up there on the mountain?"

Logan replayed parts of the story of the missing girl, Sharon Summerhill, and the Shadow Bear, leaving out his personal battles and emphasizing the rescue.

The waitress studied the lines on Logan's face. Sensing that he was reluctant to share any more details about the rescue, she changed the subject. "Are you still hearing that voice in your head?"

"That's the good part," Logan relaxed. "It's gone."

"Completely?"

"For now, I'd say yes."

"Well, that is a significant change from when you were last here. I was worried when you said it was getting stronger, telling you to do things you didn't want to do."

Logan breathed a sigh of relief, sinking down into his chair.

"Yes, the voice is gone. I'd say the rumors of my insanity have been greatly exaggerated," Logan laughed.

"So it all worked out. I'm glad for you."

"It wouldn't have," Logan said thankfully, "if not for you."

"Me? What did I do?

"The messages to Radio?" Logan pressed. "That was you, wasn't it?"

"What do you mean?"

"It's been you all along, guiding my path. I can see it now."

The waitress looked into Logan's eyes; she realized that he was now ready to accept the truth. "Yes, Logan, it was me. It was me all along."

"I knew it! But why the roundabout story? If you wanted to tell me something, why not just come out and say it?"

"You know the answer to that," the waitress said and smiled. "You need to find the path on your own, you need to figure things out. That's the way your mind works, isn't it?"

"I guess it is."

"Yes, it is. You have trust issues, you hold your heart close, and based on your history, I understand why. I thought if I gave you some clues, you would evaluate the information and come to an understanding, on your terms."

"Thank you for your guidance, and mostly for your patience."

"I'm just glad I was here for you when you needed someone to talk to."

"Me too."

"Do you think Radio will sleep now?" The waitress smiled. "I'm afraid I've been quite a bother to him."

"I think he will," Logan laughed. "He needed a job, and now he has one, thanks to you."

The waitress turned away, giving Logan some time to reflect for a moment.

"So tell me, now that you have faced your fears, what have you learned?"

"Actually, I'm still processing that one," Logan said, puzzled. "Even the things I think I've learned, it's hard for me to say them out loud. I haven't decided if I'm ready to share my personal tribulations just yet. But I wrote down what I have so far in my journal."

"Let's see what you have," the waitress said as she leaned over Logan's shoulder, her cheek next to his, and pressed the playback key.

As the computer voice spoke Logan's words, the waitress glanced out the window at Raven and Ten Bears sitting on the rocky ledge above the parking lot, hugging each other.

Chapter 58: Beacon of Light

In the silence of the abandoned Timberline Tea Haus, Logan's computer read aloud his words of understanding. He closed his eyes as the animated voice echoed through the empty room, resonating his spiritual consciousness.

"It is in our darkest hour, perched on the cliff of helplessness as we stare down into the depths of despair, that we suddenly realize one immutable truth: We are not alone in the universe. If we open our eyes and our hearts, we will see that there are others in this world that can help us. Others that have confronted their own demons and beat them back, and even though scarred from their lifelong battles, they are willing to open their hearts and offer us shelter from our own storm. It is in that moment in which we acknowledge our own vulnerability that we can find our inner strength, our voice, and our resolve to fight for the life that we deserve.

"That is not to say that the road ahead will always be smooth; it will not be. Our existence will always be a struggle, a struggle to maintain control of our life, our thoughts, and indeed, our very sanity. But when the dust finally settles on our turmoil, we will find that it has been the struggle for life that defines who we are, and who we can become. And therein lies the hidden epiphany along our rocky path; we need not walk it alone. For it is by helping others, as we both struggle at the doorstep of insanity, that we each become stronger. And it is in that instance of altruism that our destiny will be revealed, and we will find our place in this world.

"The End...for now."

Logan stared at his words on the blinking computer screen, waiting for a reaction. After what seemed to be an eternal silence, he looked up. The waitress was again gazing out the window at Raven and Ten Bears as a tear ran down her cheek.

"What do you think? Too much drama? I can change it…"

"No," the waitress sighed. "It is perfect just the way it is."

"Then why are you crying?"

"I just wish I had known you ten years ago." The waitress sniffed as she wiped a tear from her face.

"Why?" Logan pressed. He was confused.

"Oh, nothing," the waitress recovered, regaining her composure. "You should post that, what you wrote, on your blog."

"Really? Who would want to listen to my ravings?"

"There are lots of broken souls out there in the darkness, Logan, aching for the slightest glimmer of light. You can give them that hope; you are a beacon of light."

"Me? A beacon of light?" Logan blushed. "You're not serious, are you?"

"Trust me, someone out there needs to hear your words tonight. Not tomorrow, not next week when you think you have tweaked your words to be perfect, but tonight. It could make all the difference for someone at the edge of darkness."

"OK…and thanks for listening to my troubles all this time."

"We've all got them," the waitress smiled, dabbing her eyes. "Troubles, that is. Would you like some more tea?"

"No, I'm good for now; I think I just need to rest my eyes for a little while."

"You do that," the waitress put her arm around

Logan and kissed his forehead. "Sleep well, my love. May we both find the peace we seek."

Logan laid his head down on the table and smiled as he slipped back into his dream world.

Chapter 59: Lost Souls

On the rocky ledge above the dilapidated Timberline Tea Haus, Raven and Ten Bears sat in silence, watching the sun climb over the mountains, piercing through the clouds of dawn. When the last rays of light finally engulfed the snow-covered valley, Raven turned to Ten Bears, probing his eyes.

"You said there was more; what else haven't you told me? Is it about Guardian? Who is she, Grandfather?"

"Our life in this world passes quickly," Ten Bears said softly as he tapped his staff on a snow-covered rock hanging over the outcropping, admiring the multicolored lichens clinging to its side. "The Ancient Ones say that, 'It is as brief as the breath of an elk in winter.'"

Ten Bears followed the beams of light bouncing between the glistening pines, their branches swaying gently in the morning breeze. The sun shining through the icicles on the rocks created a prism of light that danced in his eyes, and then faded quickly as the light changed. "Guardian is a spirit trapped between two worlds," Ten Bears began. "She is a Wind Talker."

Raven looked down at the Tea Haus, reflecting on her grandfather's words. Since she was a child, Ten Bears had spun tales about the legends of the Ancient Ones: how they were first created in the Underworld, their struggle to emerge to the Middle World, and the quest of worthy spirits to ascend to the Sky World. She also knew of the Shadow World, the gateway between worlds, the place where lost souls would drift until it was determined which world was their rightful place.

However, now the ageless stories told around the campfire by her grandfather were not just myths, they were real, and she had become part of them. "Is Guardian the one that has been talking to Radio?"

"Yes, it was her, speaking from the Shadow World. She can see death coming for some in advance; I would not want that burden. But sometimes, a burden can be also a blessing."

"A spirit trapped between two worlds," Raven echoed. "What happened to her?"

"Ten years ago, she owned this Tea Haus; it was her lifelong dream. She had invested everything she had, and borrowed even more. But times got tough; both she and her dreams fell through the cracks of this world. The bank foreclosed and she lost everything; her life was shattered. Abandoned by all that knew her, she felt she had nothing more to live for. It was in that moment of weakness that the Shadow Bear called out to her, taunting her that the only way she could find peace was to take her own life. She contemplated suicide, but couldn't go through with it, so the Shadow Bear spun another of his webs. She called nine-one-one to report a robbery in process. When the authorities arrived, she rushed into the parking lot, waving a gun at the deputies, and they cut her down in a hail of bullets. The twisted irony of that desperate act was that her gun was not even loaded; she would never have hurt anyone else."

"That is terrible," Raven sighed.

"It was indeed. She was another troubled spirit, convinced by the Shadow Bear to surrender her life. Deep down, she was a good person that unfortunately fell victim to her inner doubts, and to the voice of the Shadow Bear."

"What happened to her then?"

"After she died, I heard her voice on the wind, calling out. She knew she had made a mistake and begged forgiveness from the Ancient Ones."

"What did you do?"

"Her spirit was submerged in the dark Pool of Purgatory, but when I heard her desperate plea, she had not yet crossed over. I sang a song of intercession to the Ancient Ones, asking penance for her deeds in this world. If given another chance, I asked, if she chose to help someone else avoid her fallen path, her spirit should be forgiven. If not, she would be swept into the River of Lost Souls to the Underworld."

"There must be thousands of spirits that cry out on the wind, Grandfather. Why did you choose to help her?"

"It was the day that I banished Logan ten years ago, and I feared I had made a terrible mistake. Even though what I did was to protect him, he could not know that. All he knew was that he tried to save you, and I punished him for it. With his parents gone, I was his only lifeline, and I turned my back on him. To him, he was abandoned, cast out by his only family for doing the right thing, at the wrong time. I am sure he hated me for what I did."

"He has carried that weight for a long time, Grandfather," Raven acknowledged.

"I know, and it was a heavy burden, wrapped in my deceit. I had to restore some sign of hope to his life, but I knew in my heart that he would not accept my help; it was too soon. So I asked her," Ten Bears said, slowly pointing to the run-down Tea Haus.

"I asked her to help him in a way that I could not. She became his Guardian, talking to him, listening to him, helping him in his struggle with the voice of the Shadow Bear. I asked her because I knew in my heart he would not listen to me."

"Logan can be pretty…stubborn sometimes," Raven agreed. "But I understand why he feels as he does; he has walked a difficult path in his life. Trust comes hard for him. If two roads separate in the woods, only he can choose which one to take."

"Yes, I feared he would be reluctant to talk directly, even to her. After what he had endured, I did not know if he was ready to receive help from anyone. So when the time came, I asked her to send messages to him through the wind, to the man in the cabin."

"So that's how Radio found Logan…"

"She needed to send her messages," Ten Bears continued, "and Niwot needed to hear them. And, as it turned out, the soldier in the cabin needed to hear them as well."

"And without them, the lost girl would have never been found," Raven marveled.

"It would seem so," Ten Bears smiled. "As the Ancient Ones say, 'The spider of truth often weaves a tangled web.'"

"So he's in there talking with her now? Guardian?"

"Yes, he is."

"But if the Shadow Bear is gone, and Logan is safe, shouldn't she be free to move on?" Raven asked, still feeling a little jealous.

"Yes, her penance has been paid," Ten Bears answered, studying Raven's discomfort. "She has helped him with his struggle, so now they are saying goodbye."

"Grandfather, when you said she has helped him with his struggle…you meant with the Shadow Bear's voice inside of him, right?"

"Yes, Raven, we all have a bear inside of us. For some, it is weak; for others, it grows to be overpowering. When Logan stabbed the Shadow Bear in the cave long ago, the Shadow Bear ripped open his chest and took his life. But in that last moment of their struggle, the blood from Logan's mortal wound mingled with the blood of the Shadow Bear, and now their spirits are forever intertwined."

"But I thought we killed the Shadow Bear? It was consumed in the fire ring."

"Yes, you killed the Shadow Bear, but you did not kill his spirit. The Shadow Bear crossed the sacred bridge and entered Niwot's spirit; it has seen through his eyes in this world. The Shadow Bear also now knows that because of Niwot's power, he could be the One. For these reasons, I fear that the Shadow Bear inside Niwot will return someday."

"Will his battle with the Shadow Bear ever end?"

"I am afraid that the Shadow Bear's spirit will always be a part of him. Niwot has two bears within his spirit: a good bear, and an evil bear, both fighting to control him. This struggle is part of who he is now, and part of who he always will be."

Raven suddenly became very quiet, realizing that although the battle with the Shadow Bear was over, the war had just begun.

"Niwot has taken part of the Shadow Bear's power, a great power that he does not yet understand. As it is with all great powers, it does not come without a cost, and without... consequences. This is part of Niwot's destiny in this world: His spirit will be locked in a constant struggle between the evil bear and the good bear inside of him."

"Which one will win, Grandfather?"

Ten Bears smiled as he put his arm around Raven. "The bear that he feeds."

Chapter 60: The One?

"The bear he feeds…" Raven said aloud, trying to make sense of all she had learned from her grandfather. "But for now," she questioned, "the voice he hears in his heart is his voice, isn't it?"

"Yes, it is."

"But Grandfather, Niwot can defeat the Shadow Bear," Raven insisted. "He has learned its weaknesses."

"And so has the Shadow Bear learned his," Ten Bears countered.

Raven thought about everything that had happened, the revelations that Ten Bears had now chosen to share, and the ache in her heart she felt for Logan.

"Is he the one, Grandfather?"

Ten Bears looked deeply into Raven's eyes, trying to read her thoughts. He was skilled at charting the precise destiny of a warrior, but even an old Medicine Man knew that affairs of the heart could be more…imprecise.

"Niwot has proven that he can battle the spirit bear within. He can walk among the undead… and now he has mastered the art of *yee naaldlooshii*. These things he has learned, and he has learned well. And yes, I believe that he has the power within him to one day carry the Thunder Stick after I am gone."

"I know that, Grandfather," Raven persisted, "he could be the One. But is he *the one*…for me?"

"My precious Raven, you are my only granddaughter," Ten Bears smiled, "my Alpine wildflower. I have shared with you the secrets of the

Ancient Ones, and you have proven yourself worthy of my trust. From the early days, it has made my heart sing to see your spirit take flight."

"Yes, I am a chosen one, you have told me that. But you know that is not what I am asking."

"You are a spirit of the Sky World, just like your mother. But if you are asking me if a warrior from the Middle World is worthy to join with a spirit of the Sky World…That is not for me to decide."

"My mother chose a warrior from the Middle World, and when she was my age as well."

"Yes, she did, and your father was a great warrior."

"I wish I'd known him," Raven said sadly.

"He was taken from our world too soon. That is why your mother entrusted me to guide both your spirit and your heart."

"So I ask you again, Grandfather. Is he…*the one*?"

"Let me ponder this," Ten Bears opined. "Alone, you and Niwot are both powerful spirits. Together, you are invincible warriors. From your battle with the Shadow Bear of the mountain, this I know. Someday, you will know if it is to be more. Only your heart can decide."

Raven put her arms around her grandfather and kissed him on the cheek.

"Why are you smiling?"

"Because my heart has decided."

Chapter 61: We're Done

Inside the Tea Haus, Logan began to slowly awaken from his dream. He wrapped his hands around his cup of tea—it was cold. Standing up to look for the waitress, he caught a glimpse out the window of Raven and Ten Bears; they were sitting patiently on the rocky ledge above the parking lot. The morning sun was glistening on the icy pine boughs, streaming a rainbow of colors that wavered in the crisp mountain air as it danced on Raven's jet-black hair.

Stepping outside the front door, Logan looked back at the Tea Haus and its blinking neon sign as it flickered in blue and white from OPEN to CLOSED. Inside, he could see that the counter was now dark, and for the first time, he noticed that there were several broken windows in the front entryway. As he walked across the parking lot to join Raven and Ten Bears, behind him, worn shingles from the roof of the run-down building blew off and tumbled down the rocky hillside.

"Are you about done with your tea time?" Raven snapped playfully.

"I think so," Logan said, looking back at the now-deserted building.

"What were you doing in there, anyway?" Raven asked as she put her hand on his cheek, looking into his eyes.

"Just gathering my thoughts," Logan said nonchalantly. "Working on my blog for my secret loyal minions."

"Are you about finished?" Raven teased.

"Almost. I just need to post my last *Truth Detector* blog entry. Apparently, there are people out there waiting to hear what I have to say."

Logan flipped open his computer, studied the blog entry for a moment, and then hit Enter.

"There," he said, as his computer made a swooshing sound. "The wisdom of the ages, off into the ether. Now I can rest easy for a while, at least until tomorrow."

"And what insights did you impart to your 'secret loyal minions?'" Raven nuzzled her face close to Logan.

"If you wish for a glimpse into the future, you'd better hope you can close your eyes…You might not like what you see."

"Truer words have never been spoken."

"And after the current crime spree, the kidnapping imposter ranger, the missing girl, and the bear?" Logan smiled. "I said, 'The End.' This chapter of my life, of *our lives*, is finished."

"I guess we all need to close a chapter every now and then," Raven sighed. "But it's not like it's an entire book…So now, we can turn the page and move on to our next adventure."

Suddenly, there was a rush of wind as the pine branches of the mountain forest creaked in the breeze. Logan looked back at the dilapidated building that was once the thriving Timberline Tea Haus and thought of the many nights he had sought the comfort of a warm cup of tea and a sympathetic ear. He held those fond memories and warm feelings close to his heart, because for him, unlike the broken-down Tea Haus, they would never fade.

"Go in peace, Guardian," Logan closed his eyes and whispered. "You never even told me your name."

He raised his hand gently in the wind, as if to wave goodbye.

"Yes, I'm done here." Logan turned to Raven, pulling her into his arms for a long embrace.

"Thank you, Guardian," Raven whispered to the breeze over Logan's shoulder, "for protecting him."

Logan and Raven held on to each other on that rocky ledge for what seemed to be both an eternity and just a moment in time. And in that moment, they each knew that from now on, both their lives and hearts forever would be intertwined.

White clouds gathered over their heads and then parted as a whirlwind spiraled upwards from the remains of the Tea Haus. In the blink of an eye, the spiritual tempest paused briefly above them, and then dissipated into the azure sky over the rocky peaks of the Continental Divide.

Raven faced Logan, locked her arms around him and looked deep into his eyes. "She's in a better place now; her spirit can rest."

Logan smiled, and then cocked his head, sensing an understanding within Raven that he had not anticipated. He'd never discussed what went on in the Tea Haus with her, or anyone else, for that matter.

Raven leaned in and kissed Logan on the cheek, resting her head on his shoulder. "In all the excitement," Raven whispered, "I didn't get to wish you a happy birthday."

"Oh...thanks."

"My birthday's tomorrow. We'll both be of age, so we can join in celebration, together. I have a special present for you, but it would be better if you opened it...in private."

"Now I'm confused," Logan blushed. "How did

you know it was my birthday?"

"A woman knows these things."

"Is there anything else I should know?"

"Yes, Niwot. The dark road you traveled with Guardian has ended, but our journey together into the light...It has just begun."

Chapter 62: Partners in Crime

"Paperwork," Sheriff Martin mumbled, completing the last of her mandatory mind-numbing forms for the single largest crime spree in recent Deadraven history.

Earlier that afternoon, deputies had discovered the body of the ranger imposter alongside the warming hut at the Spirit Lake trailhead. Their baffled report was as brief as it was mysterious: *A corpse wrapped in an Indian blanket was dropped in a snowbank*...as if it fell from the sky. No tracks were found leading to or away from the body, and other than the distant hoot of a snowy white owl, the forest was deadly silent.

"There, that's the end of it," Billie Sue sighed as she thought of Logan, checked the last signature box, and then pushed away from her desk. "I guess I owe you another one, kid."

With all bodies of the recent crime spree accounted for and the kidnapped girl safely back with her family, this case was closed. Glancing at her watch, Sheriff Martin reached for her jacket to start home for dinner with her accountant.

7:30 PM.

"Crap!" she exclaimed. "Late again."

As Billie Sue collapsed in her chair to make yet another obligatory, 'Sorry, I forgot" call, she remembered the phone number etched in her mind; the one she'd seen on Sharon Summerhill's hand in the cave.

"Who paid for the body?"

"Someone above your pay grade, Sheriff."

"Do you have a name?"

"Never had a name, just a phone number. I wrote it on my hand."

As Sheriff Martin's mind drifted from the phone number on the escaped mental patient's hand to her bloodstained shirt, she reflected on the last conversation she had with Sharon; the one right before she put a gun in her mouth and blew her brains out.

"Loose ends," Billie Sue muttered as she punched in the mysterious number on her phone, waiting for an answer. "I hate loose ends."

On the other end of the line, the phone connected and rang several times. She started to hang up, but then, an annoyingly cheerful voice chimed in, *"It's a wonderful day here at the Deadraven Winter Festival; a place where you can relax, listen to the voice of the mountain, enjoy nature, and discover your true inner self. Our offices are currently closed, but if you would like to leave a message…"*

Before the automated voice could continue, Sheriff Martin disconnected without saying a word, slumped back down in her chair, and threw off her jacket.

"Crap. When you're in a poker game and can't figure out who the mark is…it's you, genius. Enjoy your Rocky Mountain holiday—It's to die for," she mocked the voice on the phone. "Discover your true inner self? Hell, just kill it."

"You still here?" the evening dispatcher squawked, her voice echoing down the empty hallway over Billie Sue's radio, interrupting her thoughts.

"Just leaving," Sheriff Martin shouted, walking down the hall to the front desk. "Why do you ask?"

"Because your bird dog's parked out in front of the building."

"Really?"

"Been there a while. I thought he was waiting for

you or something."

Billie Sue stepped outside, and there was Logan in the light snowfall, seated on a park bench beneath a streetlight across from the skating rink. He appeared to be studying the tourists, laughing moms and dads, stumbling as they held their clumsy children learning how to ice skate for the first time. She sat down beside him in silence, catching the glow of the Winter Festival's twinkling lights as they basked in a Norman Rockwell illusion of a time gone by—a simpler, safer life.

"Did you ever get Caroline reunited with her parents?" Logan asked, without looking away from the ice rink diorama.

"Yes, I did," Sheriff Martin responded, also fixated on the skating tourists. "Mr. and Mrs. Caroline were quite thankful for the safe return of their daughter."

"Good, I bet they were relieved."

"They were so relieved that they offered me a sizable reward."

"A reward? What did you say?"

"Told them I was just doing my job. Besides, I'd have to report it…taxes and paperwork. I hate paperwork, you know."

"You should have taken it," Logan laughed, still watching the tourists stumbling about on the ice.

"Why?"

"Then you could at least afford to get that filthy shirt cleaned. Kind of scary, don't you think?"

Billie Sue looked down at her bloodstained shirt; in the excitement of the day, she'd completely forgotten about her appearance—it was pretty gruesome. "Huh? Now that would explain a few looks I got at the mayor's office."

"The mayor's office? Moving up in the world, I see."

"Yeah, when you stop a major crime spree before it craps all over Winter Wonderland, that buys you some street cred in our little Shangri-La."

"Word."

"You know what else? Life, she's funny. Seems I'm a local hero now, kind of a big deal. The mayor says I'm getting a new truck, and despite rumors to the contrary, I get to keep my job… until the next election, at least."

"Congratulations, Sheriff."

"Look," Billie Sue slid over to Logan, speaking softly. "It's not for public consumption, but I like to think of us as friends—close friends. The powers that be have been made aware of your contribution on this last case, and they'd appreciate your continued… discretion. You know, about the dead bodies and such."

"I appreciate the appreciation, Sheriff. Do I get a new truck too?"

"Well, no, there's only one hero prize for today. Maybe you can have my old truck. The ashtrays are full; I'll have to see if my accountant can write that one off."

"No worries, Sheriff. I don't even have a driver's license. But be sure to tell the powers that be thanks anyway—whoever they are."

"Hold on, don't get your panties in a knot, Sherlock, there's more. They've also authorized me to extend their gratitude…for your *continued* discretion, of course."

Logan turned away from the ice skating scene and faced Sheriff Martin with the simulated wide-eyed anticipation of a child at Christmas. "Don't toy with me, Sheriff. Are you suggesting that I'm getting a summer pass to the Ride-o-Rama? Or the Big Slide?

That's way too much fun for this city."

"Free go-kart rides for life? Dial it down a notch, partner, you'd have to marry the mayor's daughter for something that big."

"Bummer. I dig those go-karts."

"But seriously," Sheriff Martin continued, "the powers that be have freed up some budget money for my department; new equipment finally comes to the technological dark country. Encrypted videophones, you know, the ones that erase anything you send or receive in five seconds? Even Sheriff Longdick down in the valley doesn't have these babies yet. We just got them, so here you go."

"Covering your ass, are you, Sheriff?"

"Covering my ass, your ass, and the town's collective ass, actually. Seems our latest crime spree put a burr under the saddle of the council's mouthpiece about litigation, settlements, and crap like that. Some tourist spills a cup of hot coffee and they file a lawsuit these days. Just use it for all official business from now on, OK?"

"Leave no trace?"

"Yep, that's the official government mantra these days. Hard drives? My bad, they got erased. And Emails? What emails? We don't have no stinking emails."

"Denial....it's not just a river in Egypt. That's comforting."

"Hey, that's not all. You can come to work full-time now as a paid CSI, if you like. Not a volunteer intern, a certified crime scene investigator. That's a CS with a big *I*, I'm saying. You'd get a gun, a uniform, and everything. What do you think?"

"I appreciate the offer, Sheriff, but I'd be

uncomfortable joining any club that would have me as a member, especially one with a gun and a uniform. From my experience, when people strap on those things, it usually ends badly, especially for my people. No offense."

"None taken. I thought you might say that," Sheriff Martin sighed.

"Besides, don't you need a degree or something to be a *'certified'* CSI?"

"Well yes, officially, you do need *something*. But you're not the only detective in this town, remember? I got to thinking about your mysterious crime scene expertise, did some digging, and what do I find? Bada bing! I found your little off-the-books data entry job with the not-so-anonymous alcoholic coroner down in Trinity. After a little persuasion and a case of cheap scotch, he was more than happy to write a glowing letter of recommendation about your extensive forensic training—in exchange for our continued *discretion,* of course. Seems you're already on his list for Step Eight of his continuing education program, and he's up for reelection this year, you know. So there's your *something*."

"Knowledge can come from unexpected places, Sheriff. Besides, the coroner knows his secret will remain safe with me, regardless of your...persuasion."

"Really? Why?"

"Because he's not the first to fall with a bottle in his hand. We all have our demons."

"OK, counterproposal. Forget the gun and uniform, would you consider coming on as my *paid* forensics associate? In your words, you'd be like a spiritual po po consultant. Just for the cases with dead bodies, I mean?"

Logan thought about what it would be like to have a real job. Technically, he was unemployed and homeless, but for the grace of Cody Winston and the worn-out sofa in her garage. But a real job also meant real obligations; obligations where others would eventually be drawn into his world, depending on him for protection. He'd had enough trouble not getting himself killed recently; dragging others along would just put them in harm's way. And up to this point in his life, he'd always been a loner; that was just who he was. But sometimes, being the lone reed out there twisting in the cold breeze, that could get to be, well, lonely. He was at least working on that issue.

"There's a war coming, Sheriff," Logan said seriously, changing gears. "Right here in Deadraven."

"Yeah, I kind of got that feeling up there in the cave today."

"I'll do what I can, but there's no other way to say this…There will be casualties; people are going to die. Are you sure you want to be in the middle of a war?"

Sheriff Martin looked away from the happy, clueless ice skating tourists. Now it was her turn to get serious. "The only place I'm sure I *don't* want to be is in the middle of a war. If a war is coming, and I'm pretty damn sure it is, I figure I've got to choose one side or the other. Dancing around in the middle of a war…that could get a girl real dead, real fast."

"That's true. But think about it, do you really want to be by my side?"

"I wasn't really thinking of it as being by your side. I was thinking more like, you out in front, and me behind you. Like up there in the cave; you'd be my canary in the coal mine, so to speak."

"Ah, I see your point. And if the canary dies?"

"Well, that would be my cue to run like hell and get my ass out of the coal mine."

"At least you're honest, Sheriff."

"In this town, I find it's better than being dishonest—most of the time."

"Interesting advice. I think I've heard that somewhere before."

Sheriff Martin slid over close to Logan on the bench, putting her arm around his shoulder. "And since I'm dishing out free, unsolicited advice, you want another helping?"

"Why not, Sheriff? It's been one of those days."

"All right, here goes. I've been observing you for weeks now—can't help it, it's the detective in me."

"Let me guess, something is bothering you?"

"It is…"

"OK, hit me."

"How do you get by, Logan? You appear to have no visible means of support."

"Not true, Sheriff, the patrons of my *Truth Detector* website are quite generous."

"They pay you? With money?"

"I don't really need money. Let's just say that my supporters and I conduct an exchange of value, one that meets my needs, and one that requires neither the IRS nor an accountant."

"Now you're talking crazy again. No money, no mortgage, no credit card bills? A world without the IRS and accountants…I'm both frightened and excited."

"Welcome to the past and the future, Sheriff. I travel light through life—leave no trace, that's my mantra as well."

"OK, where do you live? As far as I can tell, you're homeless, other than a sofa in a mechanic's garage. You have no family, at least none that are not currently incarcerated."

"I carry those that matter to me in here." Logan pointed to his heart. "You're in here too, Sheriff."

"I'm touched, but we all need a little more, I think. Let's look at your friends. One of your best buddies is a disabled veteran, a hermit on a mountaintop with anger management problems."

"True, Radio has his issues—we all do. But if that damaged spirit wasn't my friend, we might not have made it out of that cave earlier today."

"Point well taken. Look, I'm just saying that I've been watching you for weeks, and I'm worried."

"What are you driving at, Sheriff?"

"Well, for one thing, I think you could use some, well, female companionship, for the lack of a better term."

"Companionship?"

"Yes, companionship. Hey, but not from me," Billie Sue scooted back across the bench. "I'm old enough to be your…older sister. It's just I've been thinking that a good-looking young man like you? I'm sure at times, with all the pressure of detective work and all, you need someone to…take the sharp edges off your world."

"Are we having *the talk,* Sheriff?"

"No! Well, sort of, you know what I mean. Sometimes, we all need to circle the wagons. That's kind of hard to do with just one wagon, don't you think? Never mind. Back to my detective observations, I've seen the way you and Raven look at each other. I think she's the real deal, you know. Beautiful, smart, and from what I didn't see up there in the cave, she has…other assets. And you two seem to have some kind of chemistry going on. Granted, it's a chemistry that burns things up now and then, but you can't deny that it's there. Trust me, for a guy like you, a girl like her is hard to find, especially in this alpine tourist trap. It's a little shallow here in the romantic gene pool, if you know what I mean. And besides, you two would make quite a power couple, that's all I'm saying."

"Raven is truly one of a kind," Logan played along. "Since you mentioned it, I'll give it some thought. But what about you, Sheriff? What about your…edges?"

"Me? I've got my accountant, for better or worse, and believe me, there's been some worse. But the old ball and chain can still rock my world…at least every now and then for sixty seconds or so," Billie Sue laughed.

"You know they have pills for that now."

"For the sixty-second workout? That's with the pills already."

"Oh, sorry."

"Hey, I'm not complaining; better living through chemistry. I figure a minute of good beats a lifetime of bad."

"There's a lid for every pot, Sheriff."

"So, enough of the talk; back to crime fighting. What do you think about teaming up?"

"Are you sure you want to hang out with me? These days, I seem to be attracting more than my share of…trouble, not to mention the body count."

"No problem, trouble's my middle name…well, before I changed it. Besides, I just figured that if conflict is coming to Deadraven, you and I are either going to hang together, or we're going to hang separately."

"Now you're really starting to remind me of

someone else I know, Sheriff."

"So how about it? Are you on board?"

"Maybe," Logan teased. "Let's see, you're getting a truck...What would I get? Where are my perks?"

"Perks?" Billie Sue scratched her head as she noticed a family of tourists pushing a stroller and walking their dog along the sidewalk.

"How about a canine? Search and Rescue's got dogs...We could use a homicide CSI K-9 unit up here, don't you think? You could be my dog-handling dead body consultant."

"Do you actually have a dog, Sheriff?"

"Well, no, not currently. But I have a friend who owes me a favor in a guard unit that returns next week. They have a military K-9 team that adopts out their dogs. I could pull a few strings, get you first pick."

"A K-9? A force multiplier, trained to kill on my slightest gesture? I'd have to learn Dutch, but my own dog of war? Now that would be a perk, Sheriff."

"If I get you a canine companion, are you in? Think about it, Logan. You, me, the war dog, we'd be a formidable team."

"A *he3 beniiinen*—I'd like a dog soldier."

"So will the canine companion seal the deal on our crime-fighting cartel?"

"OK, I'm in, Sheriff, but only for the dead bodies, right?"

"Of course. I'd never waste your time on anyone alive."

"When you put it that way, it's hard to resist."

"Then we have a deal?"

"Sheriff, I think this could be the start of..."

"Kick-ass K-9 crime-fighting duo?"

"I was going for a beautiful friendship, but that

works too."

"Great! Then it's settled. We'll be like high-country superheroes!"

"Wait, superheroes have cool nicknames. That could be a deal breaker, Sheriff."

"Oh, right…How about Batman and Robin? I'll be Batman."

"Too cliché. Besides, you know Batman was technically a man."

"OK, how about…the Lone Ranger and Tonto?"

"Seriously? Me as the silent Indian?"

"Sorry, my bad. Politically incorrect."

"All right, here we go. How about, 'Smokey,'" Sheriff Martin grinned, pointing to her badge, "and 'the Bear?'"

"Works for me, Sheriff," Logan smiled. "I can be the Bear."

Chapter 63: Gauntlet

"Smokey and the Bear," Sheriff Martin laughed as she stood beside Logan in the falling snow, resting her arm on his shoulder. "I think I'll order us matching sweatshirts."

"Black XL with a hoodie," Logan requested. "And a zipper front, I hate pullovers."

"OK...crap, look at the time, I've got to run. Maybe I can still make a late-night workout with that sharp-edged accountant of mine."

"On your way, Sheriff. It's unsafe to walk around with a dull knife in your pants."

As Billie Sue jogged away, Logan sat alone on the park bench across from the ice rink. Down the street, a happy family of skaters twirled and fell, laughing as the children plopped into a snowdrift to make snow angels while trying to catch snowflakes on their tongues. For the first time in ten years, Logan Lone Bear Tuu'awta's troubled spirit could finally rest. Ten Bears had accepted him back, he had friends who cared about him, and he was falling in love all over again with the beautiful young Indian girl he'd held in his heart since childhood.

Logan took a long breath and relaxed. He closed his eyes for just a moment, but the vibrating device in his jacket interrupted his peaceful interlude. "Sixty seconds already? You've got to learn to slow down and smell the roses, Sheriff."

As he clicked on the videophone, an inbound message appeared from an unknown caller ID.

"Huh. You're not the sheriff. Who are you?"

Cautiously, Logan clicked Play.

The video began in a dark forest. Furry boots stepped directly on large bear tracks that led along a snowy trail as a lone figure walked silently through the woods. There was a low growl, and the images blurred into a shaky close-up of the hairy leg of an animal. Pausing at the edge of the woods, the camera scanned a flickering light coming from a campsite just ahead.

"Creepy."

Logan fumbled in his pocket and paired his cell phone with the new device as the images continued.

Silence. The forest was devoid of life. Straining to hear any sound, Logan could barely detect muffled noises on the video as the figure crept from the woods, past a smoldering fire, and into a clearing. Beyond the fire was an old tepee covered in pine branches, protecting the entrance to a small cave beneath a rock face. Pausing outside the tepee shelter, the figure froze for a moment, listening intently for any sounds of life. After a moment, snoring and an occasional throat clearing drifted from inside the tepee. Whoever was inside, they were asleep.

"What the hell?" Logan gasped, as he now recognized the campsite in the darkness but was unable to turn away from the images on his screen.

The video continued, shuddering for a moment. There was a low, guttural snarl, and then heavy breathing as the image fogged and then cleared, refocusing once more.

Rotating down, the camera revealed a gloved, human hand protruding from an animal skin, holding a bloody knife as it slowly peeled open the flap of the shelter and stole inside. In the center of the cave, next to the glowing embers of a fire, Logan could see two bodies sleeping serenely under their buckskin blankets. One of the bodies snorted as it rolled over, causing the intruder to freeze in its tracks. From its jacket, the mysterious figure grasped a handful of dried flowers and gently sprinkled them on the smoldering embers. As a pale green haze seeped from the fire into the cave, the figure hesitated, waiting for the smoke to engulf the shelter. After several coughs, the rhythmic breathing of the two slumbering bodies resumed, confirming that the intruder had not been detected. If the sleepers managed to awaken now, they would only remember a blurry dream.

Stepping carefully, the figure bent down and held its bloodstained knife over one of the bodies, carefully pulling back the buckskin covers. The faint light of the dying fire reflected off the knife blade onto the colorful braids of a beautiful young girl's jet-black hair…it was Raven.

"No! Don't touch her!"

The figure extended its hand and slowly ran a finger along the edge of the knife blade, as if to taunt Logan, and then carefully pulled the blanket of buckskins back over Raven's peaceful face.

Guardedly retracing its steps, the intruder emerged from the tepee without a sound. It backtracked silently in the darkness until reaching the edge of the forest. Panning upwards, the camera revealed the silhouette of a hooded figure. A black mask hid the intruder's identity, except for the baleful outline of four glowing claw marks on its face.

"Show me who you are," Logan muttered, "and I will end you."

"You stumbled onto the power to enter our world," the figure whispered, "but now we can enter your world as well."

The camera panned away from the masked figure and back toward the snow-covered tepee.

"You opened the door, Niwot. Any time we want them, they are ours."

Logan stared in horror as shadows from the campfire danced across the clearing in the forest; it was the last image on his screen.

"Before the next full moon rises, you will surrender your spirit…or we will claim the lives of all you care for in this world."

After five seconds, the video faded to black and the message dissolved.

First shock, then revulsion, and finally uncontrollable rage swept through Logan's mind, burning in every fiber of his body. He shoved the videophone into his jacket and slammed his fist into the park bench, knocking it over into a snowbank. With a blood-curdling shriek, he startled the family of ice skaters across the street, sending them scrambling for the safety of their SUV in the parking lot.

As the frightened tourists sped away into the night, their headlights illuminated Logan's ashen face as he stood there, glowering up into the falling snow. His mind was spinning, his body frozen in terror.

Ten Bears had warned him long ago that his transgressions in the cave had set in motion a series of events that one day would rip apart their world, and inevitably claim many lives. The darkness inside the mountain had reawakened, and worse, it now was growing inside others. Ten Bears' dreaded vision of tragedy and sorrow…was about to come to pass.

Logan shook his head, gasping for breath, trying to regain control of his thoughts. Instinctively, he reached down and grabbed the military knife from his bootstrap, stroking the razor-sharp serrated edge of cold steel in his hand. A small stream of blood trickled down his wrist; he'd sliced open his palm to the bone, and yet, he felt no pain. Closing his eyes, Logan inhaled deeply and slipped into a dream state, channeling his father's voice from childhood.

"Remember the lessons I have taught you," Left-Hand whispered. *"Your life, and the lives of many others depend on you."*

"To protect those who count on me," Logan recounted as he slid the bloody knife back into the sheath in his boot, "to hear the inner voice of my spirit, and if need be, to kill. I remember, Father."

"A warrior is first a man of peace, Niwot, but there can be no peace when evil preys upon the helpless without mercy. Those who show no mercy deserve none in return. The tears on the graves of our ancestors have taught us a fatal lesson, Niwot. If a man is coming to kill you, get up early, and kill him first."

"I understand, Father."

"Darkness and light cannot live together; you know what must be done."

"The gauntlet has been thrown," Logan exhaled as he rubbed the throbbing scar on his chest and calmly opened his eyes.

"Long ago, I stared into the darkness of the mountain. I was alone when I looked upon the face of evil, and I was alone when I died. I will get up early and face the darkness…but this time, Father, I will not be alone."

Reaching inside his jacket, Logan retrieved the videophone, dropped it on the frozen sidewalk, and crushed it with his boot. He bent over and removed the memory card from the plastic debris, tossing the remains of the device into a nearby trash can. After righting the park bench, he dusted off the snow and sat down to scan his cellphone. Quickly browsing through the hidden applications, Logan activated an encrypted protocol. "Hey, soldier, you got your ears on?"

"You know I do, Truth Detector," Radio snapped to attention in the backwoods command center of his remote mountain cabin.

"Go secure. Too many ears."

"Transmission is clean. I'm listening."

"We've got another dead body."

"WTF?"

"One, maybe more. Probably more."

"Who?"

"Casualties of war."

"When?"

"Soon."

Epilogue

"Shape shifters, evil spirits, the undead—voices that whisper in the dark when you close your eyes. For some, these demonic apparitions are imaginary; sinister figures lurking in the shadowy corners of the mind. But for me, the demons are real. I know they're real, because I opened the door that let them in."

~ Logan, Truth Detector

The End

Join the Dead List

For more of Dead Balance, visit my website at www.garywayneclark.com. Be sure to subscribe to the Dead List and Blog feed for the latest words, music, and downloads from my frozen fortress of solitude high in the Rocky Mountains. Also, you can preview the Dead Balance Trailer, go behind the scenes of my writing process for alternative story lines and character backgrounds, as well as preview upcoming books to find out what baleful conspiracies are lurking in the shadows of my mind…

"Hoo3itoo. Koo-he-etn-oo3itoon-e3?"
A story. Should I tell you a story?
"Beneeni-noo neyoooxet cowo'oot."
I am a whirlwind passing by.
"Hehheisonoonin neniitoneino', noh hebesiibeih'in,"
Let them hear us, our fathers and our grandfathers,
"Heetihcihkoutee' hoowu3oow hiine'etiit."
So that the breath of life will endure for all time.
~ Arapaho Proverb

Like Logan, we all have our own inner demons to deal with. And as Radio warned, "Just because you're paranoid doesn't mean they're not out to get you." Until we meet in the Sky World one day my friend, I shall remain vigilant.

About the Author

Gary Wayne Clark is an engineer by training, a venture capitalist by trade, but a storyteller at heart. With interests as varied as science fiction, movie soundtracks, poetry, and photography, many divergent projects have sprung to life from his frozen fortress of solitude high in the Rocky Mountains of Colorado.

His sci-fi novel series, "The Devolution Chronicles," is an epic journey from a post-apocalyptic Earth to the planet of Niburu, where the reader is asked: "What if there was a world where man no longer reigned, and evolution ran backwards?" His haiku/photography series, "High Country Haiku," is a photographic journal of life above eight thousand feet in the Rocky Mountains of Colorado. It started as a way to capture the native spirit of a simpler life in America's high country, but devolved into something deeper, something more spiritual, and in the end, provided a glimpse of the path to enlightenment.

As a member of the Grammy® Recording Academy, the hallmark of his stories are the critically-acclaimed companion soundtracks by his band, *Earamas*™. Songwriters Gary Wayne Clark and Glen Dale Spreen provide an island of uniqueness amid an ocean of conformity. Together they have quietly been weaving an unexpected genre bending musical tapestry that stretches the boundaries of the imagination. With four albums and two singles, their music can be heard streaming from the cloud in eighty-five countries around the world.

When Gary's not wandering the Trail of the

Ancients, exploring the ruins of Chaco Canyon, or traveling among the Hopi and Navajo tribes to share stories, he lives in the high country of Colorado on his ranch with his wife Jillaine, a Great Doodle named Neli, and the spirit of his shape-shifting interspecies translator, a telepathic Great Dane named Raz.

Follow

For words, music, poetry, photography, and more, you can follow Gary Wayne Clark on most social networks.

Facebook

Twitter

Google +

ReverbNation

More

Books by Gary Wayne Clark...

The Devolution Chronicles: Passage to Niburu

The Devolution Chronicles: Rise of the Chimera

"When nuclear Armageddon spawns a post-apocalyptic dystopian future, the surface of the Earth is obliterated. A band of unlikely survivors fleeing the destruction are launched into space, and the adventure catapults them into worlds unknown. Unaware of the cosmic forces in play, a bounty hunter tracking his nemesis weighs revenge against survival when he stumbles into a world where he soon discovers that evolution...runs backwards."

High Country Haiku: Winter

High Country Haiku: Winter

"When a photographer trades the urban jungle of Los Angeles for winter in the Rocky Mountains of Colorado, poetry is revealed among hushed footfalls on new fallen snow."

Emonesia (Interactive Musical Songbook)

"Behind the music, lyrics, images, videos, and songwriting notes, Emonesia invites the reader backstage for an intimate look inside the creative world of the songwriting duo known as Earamas™, critically acclaimed as 'brilliant composers and undisputed geniuses behind the controls of a soundboard.'"

Music by Gary Wayne Clark

Emonesia (Album)

"Emonesia is a musical journal of love lost, desperately sought, and ultimately found. Described as 'Nashville meets Hollywood for love songs and stories in a soft rock style with a country twist,' it is the first album recorded and produced by Gary Wayne Clark and Glen Dale Spreen."

Passage to Niburu (Album)

"Emotive orchestral soundtrack fused with ambient cinematic sci-fi storytelling, hybrid electronica, and a film noir theatrical element of prophetic visions from the multiverse."

Rise of the Chimera (Album)

"Gary Wayne Clark and Glen Dale Spreen are brilliant composers and undisputed geniuses behind the controls of a soundboard. Rise of the Chimera is powerful, haunting, beautiful, and unique. The sound quality is astounding, and this is an album that can be listened to many times, each time yielding some new and previously undiscovered treasure." Rhonda Readence, ReviewYou CD Reviews - Rating: 5 stars (out of 5)

Day by Day (Single)

"Singer / songwriter ballad in a "Nashville meets Hollywood" soft rock style with a Country twist."

Lonely With Someone I Love (Single)

Eclectic Texas blues artist Tommie Lee Bradley teams with Grammy® Recording Academy songwriters Gary Wayne Clark and Glen Dale Spreen (a.k.a. Earamas™) for the soulful country ballad, "Lonely With Someone I Love."

Acknowledgments

Thanks to all those living in the shadow of the Continental Divide who confided their own real-life mysteries of the many strange, unexplained events that somehow get swept under the rug of truth. From Lew's diligent monitoring of all harmonic frequencies, Deanna's tinkering with the big ruckus conspiracy in my mind, to law enforcement, medical personnel, dentists, park rangers, and the everyday town folk I have swapped stories with here in the gateway to Rocky Mountain National Park...You know who you are. Cheers to Alison at FirstEditing and a salute to my wordsmith wingman and editor Mark Hooper who has been with me since Commander Ryker fled the post-apocalyptic dystopia of Confederation Zone 51 for planet Niburu, twenty-five years in the future.

As a writer, my mind habitually traverses story lines driven by a transcendent connection with the spiritual beliefs of Native Americans. Their respect for the earth, for nature, and their celestial bond and nexus with the universe has always felt to be a comfortable place in my soul. Admittedly, my illusory linkage was partially nurtured by an improbable tale told for generations, of a young woman who fell in love with a famous war chief, and when forbidden to consummate their romance, secretly became his bride and mother to his children. A dubious ancestral story, just a folktale really, until recently I received the results from a DNA test and discovered my own Native American ancestry. People say that buried inside every folktale is an imaginary kernel of truth. For me, this scientific revelation and mystical reconnection has opened a door to many plausible possibilities.

I owe particular thanks to my brothers, the Native American people of the Arapaho, Hopi, Navajo, Ute, and Shawnee Nations, and especially Gary Tso, the Left-Handed Hunter, for the friendship, medicine, and tales we have shared over the years.

The inspiration for my writing is encapsulated in the words of the Ancient Ones in a Hopi proverb that speaks to my own personal truth:

"He who tells the stories…rules the world."

**